The night-shrouded Earth formed a velvet-black backdrop. Here and there cities glowed; tiny sparks of lightning showed in the storm off Portugal.

"Ready?"

"Give me a moment," Marion said happily. "I never could resist a sunrise."

The sun flared into view: a sudden white crescent glowed along the Earth's eastern rim. A tiny brightness showed above Iran, floated into the daylit area and was gone.

"Thomas, did you see anything out there? I thought I caught a flare of some kind."

"Where?"

"High in the atmosphere . . . Janet, did you see it?"

"No."

Thomas whistled low, in irritation. "All right, I'll take a look." He had almost reached the mating rings, where the ion drive joined the cable pod. Now his backpack jets flared and he veered away, behind *Gabriel.* "Okay, where?"

Marion sounded almost petulant. "It was there. I saw it."

Thomas closed his eyes and counted to five. "Right. Now we can get on with the—" The mating rings exploded, searing his vision white as the world turned to fire and pain.

THE DESCENT OF

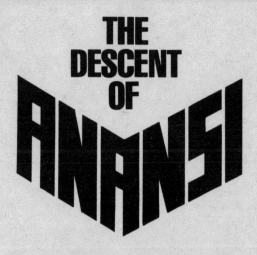

LARRY NIVEN
& STEVEN BARNES

A TOM DOHERTY ASSOCIATES BOOK

THE DESCENT OF ANANSI

Copyright © 1982 by Larry Niven and Steven Barnes

A TOR Book

First printing, September 1982

ISBN: 0-812-54700-4
CAN. ED.: 0-812-54701-2

Cover art by: Howard Chaykin

Printed in the United States of America

TABLE OF CONTENTS

Members of the Brasil Techimetal-Electromotores:
  Jorge Xavier (Vice-President)
  Lucio Giorgi (Engineering)
  Edson da Silva (Finance)
  Djalma Costa (Industrial Relations)
  Luisa (receptionist, BTE building)
  Castellon (President)
  Eric Burgess (Captain, *Brasilia*)
  Ricardo Diaz (Copilot, *Brasilia*)
  Correro (Psychologist & Missions
    Specialist, *Brasilia*)

UMAF personnel:
  Resa Mansur
  Hassan Ali Hoveida

Falling Angels Enterprises personnel:
  Fleming (President)
  Miss Ellinshaw (Air Quality Control)
  Janet De Camp (Pilot, *Anansi*)
  Thomas De Camp (Ion drive technician, *Gabriel*)
  Mrs. Kelly (Fleming's personal secretary)
  Marion Guiness (Copilot, *Anansi*)
  Dr. Dexter Stonecypher (Metallurgist)
  Tim Connors (Ion drive technician and pilot, *Michael*)

Oyama Construction personnel:
  Takayuki Yamada
  Retsudo Oyama

One

HIGH FINANCE

On October 16, 1970, the Comsat Board of Directors declared a dividend of 12.5 cents per share. This was approximately one million dollars, and represented a milestone: the first money made by the general public from a space enterprise.

It took a little over six years for Comsat to go from initial start-up to a dividend-paying operation.

The Brazil Techimetal-Electromotores building was the second tallest in all of Sao Paulo, a glistening golden spire that sprouted from a cluster of drab five-story structures, an egotistical giant among dwarves.

Xavier parked his Mercedes in the underground parking structure, and took Yamada up to the thirty-first floor in a public elevator. There they changed to a security elevator.

Jorge Xavier stood perfectly erect, and nearly a foot taller than his companion. His face was dark, his hair thick and fluffy and prematurely white; he was altogether a tailor's dream. Now his generous mouth was drawn into a slender line, his brows wrinkled in concentration. He asked—in English; he had learned that Yamada's Portuguese was poor—"You are sure of the amount?"

"Absolutely. Oyama Construction wants the cable at all costs. The Trans-Korea bridge will make their reputation."

Xavier slammed the edge of his palm into the elevator wall, swearing in Portuguese. "I know, I know. It is why we must have it. With the Stonecypher Cable in our hands, we can force Oyama construction into a merger. Such a merger would combine the raw materials and manpower available to BTE with the technical resources and world respectability of Oyama Construction. With terms favorable to both sides, such a merger could be—" he groped for words. "I do not care what it takes. We will have that cable."

"Your company president. Your Senhor Castellon. He will not match Oyama's bid?"

"Castellon is a sick old man. He spends half of the year in Caxambu, drinking the waters to heal a faulty liver. His problem is not in the liver—it is in the heart. He has no heart for a gamble."

An electric-eye scan of the BTE executive's identification card admitted them to the fifty-fourth floor. Yamada stepped out and smiled reflexively at the pleasant softness of the carpet. He said, "And you do?"

"I would not have brought you here otherwise. I, and a few others in my company, we have the heart. We are young, and strong. We will gamble."

Yamada wondered, too late, if it had been wise to betray Oyama Construction to this man. He was suddenly very aware of what he himself was gambling. Income, reputation, honor, freedom . . . if he lost.

The BTE executive suite was as luxurious as practicality would allow. Muted music flowed from the inner walls, and many of the outer walls were gold-tinted plastic. The tinting reduced the glare without obstructing the view of the city. It was a view worthy of appreciation, a vista of silver and red buildings sparkling in the sun almost as far as the eye could see.

The receptionist was alert and smiling a greeting as the elevator door slid open. *"Boa tarde, Senhor Xavier."*

"Boa tarde, Luisa. Apresento-lhe o Senhor . . . " he turned to Yamada apologetically. "Excuse me. Luisa, this is Mr. Yamada. We will be in conference. Call Mr. da Silva, Mr. Costa, and Mr. Giorgi. Have them come to my office. *Obrigado.* Mr. Yamada? This way, please."

Xavier led the slender Oriental down the hallway and steered him around a right corner. This corridor ended in a huge oak-panelled door with the name J. Xavier centered on a rectangle of brass. The door swung open without a sound, and they entered.

There was a large conference desk in the front part of the office with a setup for videophone conferences. Yamada doubted that Xavier would want the contents of this particular conference broadcast over any line, no matter how secure.

"Please. Be seated. Drink?" Yamada shook his head *no*, accepting the invitation to sit. Xavier busied himself at a small wetbar, coming back with a short glass of ice and clear liquid garnished with a twisted slice of lime.

He sat across from Yamada, sipped his drink and gazed at him speculatively. Yamada felt naked, stripped to the skin and then flensed to the bone. Xavier probed and examined and weighed, finally laying the meat and organs back in place, slipping the skin back onto the body.

No Japanese would have stared so. The room's silence was oppressive, and Yamada fought to escape that gaze, to break contact with those bottomless black eyes. He found a painting to look at, a garish thing of oranges and blacks. Concentric rings of color surrounded plastic bubbles that rose inches out from the canvas, sprays of yellow arcing through the black background like comets through space.

A name clicked in his mind. "This is your Mr. Castellar's work, is it not?"

Xavier smiled, some of the coolness leaving his face. "Yes. You know our painters? He was one of the finest. Emilio Castellar dreamed of space when much of our country was trying merely to enter the industrial age. A man of vision."

The office door opened, and two men entered, followed a moment later by a third. One of them was Xavier's height, a fraction over six feet, but heavy in the stomach and thighs. He nodded without speaking. Xavier filled the silence. "This is Mr. da Silva. Edson da Silva."

The second was a small, neat man with a beard that had been trimmed to a razor point. His hazel eyes seemed to be in constant quick movement. His skin was lighter than Xavier's or da Silva's. He sized Yamada up in two intense seconds, then stretched out his hand. "Djalma Costa," he said. "Djalma with a *D*."

"Takayuki Yamada." Yamada turned to the third man, noting the limp, and the silver wolf's head cane that corrected it. "And of course you are Mr. Giorgi. Lucio Giorgi."

Giorgi was as tall as da Silva, but much thinner. His eyes were hollow, and the skin on his face was stretched taut over the bones, as if a long illness had stripped away the fat. Giorgi nodded with satisfaction and spoke with excellent, though accented, English. "I see that news of my accident precedes me."

"We were interested in your work on the Parana Dam project. Of course, when the scaffolding collapsed, we knew that the famous Giorgi had been the only survivor."

"I am perhaps too old to continue on-site inspections."

"If this project is as successful as we hope, we will definitely desire your expertise." They shook hands, and all five men were seated.

There was a moment of uncomfortable tension. Then Xavier cleared his throat and slapped his palms on the table. "Well, Mr. Yamada. If you would be so kind as to share your information with us."

"Certainly." All hesitation had left him now. He swung his briefcase up to the table and dialed its five-digit combination. There was a sharp click, and Yamada eased it open and removed a thin folder of papers. He locked the case and set it on the floor.

Yamada thumbed through the folder, talking to himself in barely audible Japanese. "Ah, yes. I trust that I do not have to fill you three gentlemen," nodding in the direction of the newcomers, "in on much of the background material?"

"Skim through to today's business," Xavier suggested.

"Agreed. The item of interest is a cable recently extruded by Falling Angel Enterprises. Put as simply as possible, the cable is a strand of single-crystal iron filaments locked in an epoxy matrix." He looked up at them with a distracted look on his face. "It is eight-tenths of a millimeter thick and fourteen hundred kilometers long. All preliminary tests indicate that it is much stronger than Kevlar, at least ten or twenty times stronger."

His eyes slid over a page and a half of notes. "Suffice it to say that the . . . ah . . . delicate situation existing between America's National Aeronautics and Space Administration and Falling Angel Enterprises has severely limited buyers for the cable."

Da Silva nodded enthusiastically. "This is true. Pressure from the U. S. of A. has caused four nations to drop out of the bidding, Great Britain just this morning."

"Saving face," Costa laughed. "They knew they would be outbid. Quitting now earns them a few points in the eyes of the Americans." There was a twist on the word "American," as if he was sharing a private joke. "No. We and the Japanese are the only ones remaining in the bidding."

"I think that I can guarantee that Oyama Construction will win the bid. The Bridge project is entirely too important."

Xavier caught his breath. "How high is Oyama going?"

"One hundred and eighty million dollars."

There was a hiss of exhaled breath, and Costa cursed vividly. "He's insane . . ."

"No," Xavier said, his voice a solid weight in the room. "It is one of a kind. A thousand miles of the strongest cable ever produced by man. An option on the next five thousand to be produced. Oyama is taking the kind of gamble that Castellon would have taken twenty years ago, before he lost his *ovos*. Unlike any material ever produced on earth, now in orbit around the Moon, waiting for someone with the will to defy the stockholders and the U. S. of A."

"There is no hope that your Mr. Castellon will commit more funds to the project?"

"None. One hundred million is as high as he is prepared to go."

"Then Oyama will win the bid."

The five men looked at each other, saying nothing. Costa watched Xavier carefully, watched him turn to Giorgi and measure his words before speaking. "Lucio. In your opinion, how important is that cable to the construction of the Japan-South Korea bridge?"

Giorgi's hollow, pale face took on some color as he sat forward, fingers twining animatedly. "Mr. da Silva will correct me if I am wrong, but Oyama Construction is overextended financially. If the project is successful, Oyama will be in an exceedingly advantageous position. If it fails, or if the Bridge goes disastrously over budget, they will be in considerable difficulty. Certainly the present administration of the company would undergo considerable upheaval. Therefore, they need the Cable. Even at the cost of one hundred and eighty million dollars, it is cheap.

They will save money, time, and establish a permanent advertisement for their most advanced engineering techniques. Oh, yes, they need it. Oh, yes."

Xavier's eyes were cold and calm. "Well, then. If it is certain that Oyama needs the Cable, then we can proceed with Phase Two. Again, Mr. Yamada?"

The Japanese swallowed, stepping over the edge of a mental cliff, trusting that there was water at the base. "I can supply you with course data for the Space Shuttle *Anansi*. With this information, you will know where the vehicle is during every second of its descent to Kwanto spaceport. If all the other elements are in readiness, interception will be possible."

"Excellent." Xavier took a thoughtful sip of his drink, eyes focused on the wall behind Yamada. "Giorgi. You are sure of your pilots?"

"Their loyalty is to me. To us. They understand their reward for efficiency and discretion will be . . . handsome. We will need 48 hours start-up time."

"Costa? Your friends in the UMAF?"

"Ready and eager. It has been a dry time for them, and a headline of such magnitude will do much to revitalize the organization."

"I try never to denegrate our . . . allies . . . but one would think that these people would forget the Zionites and find themselves another war. It has been sixty years."

Costa laughed loudly, the laughter dimming to chuckles, then a private smile as no one else joined in. Xavier drummed his fingers on the table. He said, "It is a holy war. Soldiers in a holy war win or die. They do not seek new wars. Mr. da Silva?"

"As of today, for a short operation, I believe that we can divert nearly eight million dollars from the central computer without any danger until the July audit." Da Silva twisted slightly in his chair and wiped a thin sheen of perspiration from his forehead. Yamada noted that it wasn't warm in the conference room.

"Today is November the Seventeenth. That gives us almost seven months. By that time, it will all be over, one way or the other. Well, gentlemen . . . there is the gamble: Disgrace and prosecution, or control of Brasil Teci-metal-Electromotores."

Again, there was no sound in the room, except for the subdued hum of the air conditioner. Then Giorgi cleared his throat and spoke. "I myself have always been a gambling man."

There was a murmur of agreement, and Yamada joined in quietly.

"Good," said Xavier. "Then, gentlemen: let us drink to our venture." He rose halfway from the table, then turned back, his expression of content tinged with doubt. "Lucio," he asked, "Are you quite certain about the missile? We can trust the UMAF to operate it properly?"

"We will have our own man on hand to supervise."

"Good, good. It is best not to take chances." He dusted his hands against each other. "Well. That drink, eh?"

Two

GRAND THEFT

A dull murmur wound its way through the audience, a murmur which could erupt into a roar at any moment. Thomas De Camp shifted uncomfortably and whispered, "I don't like this." His small dark eyes flickered around the room. "I really don't need to be here. All they need from me is my vote."

Janet De Camp squeezed his hand, brought her lips close to his ear. "Look at these people. Most of them don't want to be here, either. They just want it to be over, one way or the other. We need you here, Tommy."

He looked down at their locked hands, her pale fingers forming a crisscross pattern against his dark brown skin, and sighed, knowing she was right. *Someone* had to be here, someone who cared. He just wished that it didn't have to be him. Janet pressed his hand again, then released it. Her ice-blue eyes were alive with eagerness, and the contrast to his own feelings was as marked as their physical contrast: her Nordic blood against his African and Oriental features, her five foot eight against his five and a half. The differences went deeper, deeper than he wanted to think about now.

A circular magnification screen glowed at one end of the Space Shuttle external tank that served as a meeting hall. Nobody had used chairs for free fall since Skylab. The hundred-and-fifty foot tank was a maze of netting. One hundred and eighty barefoot audience members clung to the lines by fingers and toes, like flies in a spiderweb, with this one difference: their feet all pointed in one direction, a tacitly agreed-upon "down."

The magnification screen was still blank: Fleming, the head of Falling Angel Enterprises, had yet to mount the podium.

There was a trickle of excitement from the back of the meeting hall, and De Camp turned his head in time to see Fleming and one of his aides gliding up the center safety line. He might have been going hand-over-hand up a rope, but no Marine fitness instructor ever floated "up" a line so effortlessly. Reaching the screen, Fleming unhooked his safety and nudged himself into position, refastening himself to the podium. His aide fastened herself to a nearby strand and handed him his briefcase.

Fleming cleaned his glasses, his gently humorous face seeming too long until he slipped them on again. "Good afternoon. I know that seems a cruel joke to those of you on the 2200 shift, but bear with an old man, eh?"

A tension-easing chuckle warmed the room as Fleming inserted a cartridge into the podium and flashed through his notes. A brawny Solar Satellite tech in front of the De Camps unhooked his fingers from the web and stretched his arms. "This isn't going to be good," he said to no one in particular. "Fleming is smiling."

"Give him a chance," Thomas said, before he realized he was speaking aloud. The tech turned and looked at him with a bemused smile.

Fleming took his usual position at the mike, hands braced at the side of the podium, pulling *down* to make his own gravity. "Can all of you hear me? Good, good." He arched his back, and long muscles flexed. He spent more time in the centrifugal-gravity of the administrative offices than anyone in Falling Angel. He looked every inch the patriarch, and the fatigue lines in his face only strengthened the image. "Well, I have just finished a short conversation with our friends in NASA." He let the ripple of laughter run its course. "Not totally to my surprise, they still refuse to deal with us. I believe that the most popular term being applied to us is 'lunatic pirates.'"

A thin woman—her name escaped Thomas, although he knew she worked in Air Quality—raised her hand. "And why shouldn't they call us pirates?" she asked testily. "Everything that we have up here was paid for by the taxpayers of the United States. As far as they're concerned, we're robbing them."

"Miss Ellinshaw," Fleming said, adjusting his glasses, "the last thing in this world I intend is to turn my back on the American people. You must understand that the incorporation of Falling Angel was a matter of much debate and controversy before any announcement was made."

"You're still stealing." Her words were set in concrete, beyond argument, and De Camp was suddenly glad he had never had to requisition a recycler filter from her.

Fleming's face reddened when she said that, and his teeth were set tightly, little muscles at the hinge of the jaw twitching. He had risked health and reputation to build Falling Angel from a single spacecraft in close orbit around the Moon, to a collection of clumped space junk, to one of the finest laboratory complexes in the world. He had supervised the expansion personally, scuffling and battling every inch of the way with the Earthlocked NASA honchos. Balding now, eyes weakened from long hours pouring over computer displays, Fleming had personally suited up and led rescue operations, supervised the construction of the big mass driver in *Mare*

Crisium, and for the past twelve years had poured his life and organizational genius into Falling Angel. At another time, this same roomful of people might have soberly discussed spacing Ellenshaw for those words.

Today, there was merely a whisper of assent.

"Stealing?" Fleming asked softly. "I think not. In the twelve years that Falling Angel has been in existence, we have repaid the original investment in our facility one and one half times. Adjusting for inflation and interest on the original 'loan,' it is arguable that we still owe the United States a few million dollars. Believe me—every effort will be made to set this right. The truth of the situation is that unless we are freed from the present crippling bureaucracy, we will soon be unable to operate at all.

"Friends, we are a quarter of a million miles from the folks who do most of the voting. To us—to each other, here—Falling Angel is our whole world. To America, we are a few hundred people engaged in an exotic operation which has taken twelve years to break even. When the next budget cutback comes down the pipe, most voters will vote for something they can see and touch and understand. And one day, without any noise, Falling Angel will die, like so much of our space program." He paused, and it was easy now to feel the weariness in him. Thomas chewed at the inside of his cheek, finding it difficult to watch. "And like so many other noble efforts, so many other dreams, one day we'll all pack up and go home."

Fleming gripped the side of the lectern and leaned forward, anger alive in his voice. "I'm an old man, and I've given my life to Falling Angel and the technology that build her. I'm too damned old to start over, and too damned mean to take this thing gracefully. We're going to show the American people that we can survive as a business, that we can make money—for *them*. If we can't appeal to their hearts, we'll try their wallets, but we're *not going to lose*. We need things that only Earth has, and Earth needs things that only we can make. We're Americans here, but we're something else, too. We're the future. If America doesn't believe in her future anymore, then maybe it's up to us to show her we're not dead yet."

At least half of the audience applauded loudly as Fleming pushed himself back from the podium and scanned them. Janet De Camp whispered to her husband: "Round one for the Good Guys."

The floor was opened for discussion, and controversy raged. Could Falling Angel truly survive as an independent? Could NASA or the American military retaliate?

The second question Fleming answered immediately. "If you ask that, you don't understand the situation. We aren't sitting on top of a diamond mine up here. At present we are considered a marginal enterprise. While we *do* have products we can sell, Congress will expect us to collapse without their support. When we don't, they may have some ideas about taking over, but remember: the real wealth of Falling Angel is its experienced personnel. At worst they might make an example of me and a few of my most conspicuous officers. The rest of you will be even more valuable to them than you are now.

"The American voter can see Falling Angel if he owns a telescope and knows enough to aim it right when we're rounding the edge of the Moon. *That* voter is fairly rare, and he's on our side anyway, and what does he see? A junkyard of expended Shuttle main tanks. Hardly something worth fighting over. What else? A fleet of six antiquated Space Shuttles, two of which NASA has already confiscated because they were on the ground, and three cesium-fueled ion drive tugs capable of moving them between Earth and Lunar orbit."

There were a few more minutes of talk, then Ellinshaw raised her hand and stood again. "Mr. Fleming," she said, "I move that we put this to a vote *now*."

He nodded. "All right. Seconded?"

The silence lasted too long for Thomas' comfort, and he raised a stocky arm. "Seconded."

"Then a vote it is. All in favor of independence for Falling Angel?"

For an instant there was no movement in the room, then hands began to rise like sprouted seedlings, until just under half of the personnel had raised their arms. There was a quick count.

"Opposed?"

Fleming's assistant counted again, and handed her tally up to the administrator. He looked it over with a neutral expression. Janet's face flattened with dismay. "We lost." She sounded numb.

"Wait. It's not over yet."

Fleming handed the tally back, then addressed them. "All post-essential personnel and lunar personnel have submitted proxies. The initialed vote sheets have been tabulated, and are available for inspection in my office. The official tally is: Independence, 147, Opposed, 142. The motion passes."

There were a few cheers, but also a rumbling undercurrent of discontent. Fleming raised his hand for attention. "Those of you who voted to remain under control of NASA may leave Falling Angel if you wish. We have made arrangements to ferry you back. This will relieve you of any fear of prosecution. Those of you who stay, well, I hope you know how badly we need each and every one of you, now more than ever. Let it be a matter between you and your conscience. Just remember—it's your future we're fighting for."

Fleming left the lecturn to scattered applause, much of the audience already divided into percolating knots of controversy.

Thomas turned to his wife, unhooking fingers and toes from the net. "Well, that's that."

"We did it, Tommy." She grinned broadly. "Look at this. Are you sure you don't want to stick around? You won't find action like this out in the Belt." Her smile was a mask, her voice part wheedle and part sorrowful acceptance.

"I need quiet. Makes it easier to do the job. Anyway, I'll be wherever the ion drives are. I've done my part here."

Their eyes met and locked, and Janet tore hers away first. She tugged at him as he launched himself towards the safety line. "See you for dinner?"

There was quiet humor in the dark mongol face, humor that rose to a smile. "Sure. I'll be in the shop if you need me."

She nodded, watched him swim up the line with the smile fading from her lips. For a moment her vision misted, then she shook her head clear. "No time for that," she said fiercely, quietly. Then: "Damn it, there's no time for anything, anymore." Janet flexed the cramp from her fingers and joined the exodus, dozens of barefooted figures waiting for a place in line, heading for the locks.

Three

THE AUCTION

Most of those leaving the meeting hall donned pressure suits or took one of the connection tubes, but the administrator of Falling Angel had a scooter waiting. The pressurized three-man vehicles were in short supply, and generally reserved for the repair crews.

Fleming eased into the control seat and waited for his assistant to climb in next to him. Mrs. Kelly was a chunky woman on the far end of forty, married to one of the solar engineers. Bright, competent, and fiercely loyal to Falling Angel Enterprises. But she never moved quickly enough for Fleming's taste. After more than thirty months at the facility, she still wasn't used to zero gravity. No problems with it, in fact just the opposite.

Unless there was a specific demand for speed she seemed to linger over each separate movement, savoring it.

She had buckled herself in and sealed the door. Fleming broke anchor manually and they floated away, accelerating.

The universe was silence and razor-edged shadow as they cruised along the sprawling structure of Falling Angel. A score of Shuttle external tanks were splayed out in orbit around the Moon, serving as a basis for the industrial complexes that served the needs of America, the Soviet Union, and the European Combine.

Suddenly Fleming's crow's-feet squeezed flat, and he pointed at a dimly lit rounded object, like a water-smoothed rock equipped with tailfins. "Notation, Kelly. Find out why Strickland still has men working on the cable re-entry package. I was told it was ready to go."

She nodded, scribbling, glad that he had broken the silence. "What do you think about the meeting?" They were passing through a cluster of Shuttles. She ticked the names of the winged boxcars as they passed: *Susanoo*, *Lucifer* (that name had proven an ill omen: on its thirteenth descent to Earth, the landing gear exploded on impact. Only fast action by the fire crews, and a shock-absorbing restraint wall made of Dexter Stonecypher's "enhanced" fiberglass, had saved lives and cargo.), *Haephestus*, and the newest addition, *Anansi*.

Fleming said nothing for a few seconds, only the flickering dim lights of the computer display bringing his face to life. He watched the spinning bulk of the exercise room pass to their right. "We'll make it. We'll be down to half strength, but the people who stay, they're the real workers. The deadweight just voted itself out." His hands played delicately over the controls, and his voice never wavered. It took someone very familiar with his ways to sense the bitterness in him, but Mrs. Kelly was that close, and more. "We can count on them. You'll see." His eyes never left the shadow-crested shapes rising beneath and around the scooter.

He smiled now, and she was happy to see it was his private smile, not the one he pulled out and glued on for meetings. She could imagine him smiling thus at an hour's worth of sand castle, fifty years ago. "You know . . . sometimes when I'm sitting at my desk it gets easy to be abstract about this . . . junk sculpture. It's just so much metal and plastic tubing, consuming so many pounds of oxygen and water, and so many millions of dollars a month. A thing. But here—" She could see his eyes building infrastructures as they scanned the complex. Building, changing, improving . . . and never satisfied.

The scooter went into an approach path for the administration buildings: a flat disk connecting three Shuttle tanks. The tanks rotated about the axis of the disk, providing "gravity" for the offices. The center disk housed the filing and supply warehouse.

He docked without a bump, and Kelly
sealed their door on, waiting for Safety to
approve and admit them to the tiny airlock.
She barely noticed the sensation of weight returning as she lifted Fleming's briefcase from
the rear seat and carried it off with her.

The alarm in Kelly's wristwatch buzzed
until she flicked it off. "Looks like we're just
in time," she said, helping Fleming from the
scooter. "The calls are coming through."

"Good, good. Put them on hold. We'll be
there in a minute." The inner lock opened and
let them through. The hallways and corridors
were largely plain, but not severely so. Kelly
could remember infinities of bare plastic trim
laid on foam steel. Now, the niceties of
gracious living were creeping aboard. The
crew, invited to assist with the decorating,
had responded with a generous sampling of
their talents: oilpaintings, sculpture, an
achingly beautiful tinsel and blown glass
mobile. There were many moonscapes, including one spectacular view of the Apennine
mountains which had won second prize in the
Venice Arts Festival, Earthside. Kelly still
remembered passing the hat to pay for the
shipping space aboard a Shuttle.

Closer to the center of the hub the floor was
carpeted in Velcro, but that was unnecessary
out at the edge, with two-thirds Earth gravity
to hold a traveler down.

The office section was largely deserted,

which made the narrow hallways seem more spacious. It was a feeling to cherish and to dread. If this desperate plan didn't work . . .

Fleming was reaching for the doorknob when it slid away under his hand. Dr. Stonecypher popped his head out, bending so that his greying hair barely grazed the top of the six-foot doorframe. His thick eyebrows knitted in perplexity. "There you are, Benjamin." He checked his watch with poorly concealed irritation. "I was beginning to worry." He moved his towering frame aside to let them pass, moving with the strange, disjointed grace of a praying mantis. Dr. Stonecypher was one of the original Falling Angels, and held the record for time spent in null-grav, beating out the nearest contender, a Russian communications specialist in orbit around earth, by several thousand hours.

He virtually lived in the Metallurgy and Special Projects lab he had built over the past fifteen years, spinning out the miracles that made Falling Angel what it was: the most advanced zero-gravity research and production facility in the world. During that time, he had undergone one of the rarer effects of long-term work in space. Unhampered by gravity's fierce and constant tug, fed a constant high-mineral diet to counteract the negative calcium transport often experienced by long-term astronauts, his skeletal structure had experienced a second anabolic stage. The bones were growing again. He was nearly seven inches taller than the Stonecypher who had matured on Earth, and the medics were franklly baffled as to when the sixty-three-year-old metallurgist could expect it to stop.

Eight years older than Fleming, Stonecypher was one of the few people who addressed him by name, and the only man Kelly had ever seen upbraid him. Fleming took it well. There was only one Dexter Stonecypher, and his expertise in a very special field was irreplaceable.

"Come, come," Dexter said, shooing Fleming along with a thin-fingered hand. Stonecypher walked along behind him with the painstaking delicacy he always adopted on his infrequent sojourns into the centrifugal zone. "I still have to supervise mating of *Gabriel* and the cable pod. Special Projects is going crazy over dead rats and dead *fleas* for gosh sake. Mark my word—you'll push me too far one day. Dead rats indeed. And oh," he added almost as an afterthought, "We're holding Japan and Brazil on the line."

Fleming took the briefcase from Kelly and took his position at the conference table. "Let's not fall apart now, Dexter. A bit of teasing never hurt a sale. If it's worth buying, it's worth waiting for."

"An unexpected result of overexposure to moonlight," Stonecypher growled to Kelly as he took his place next to Fleming. He looked down at the top of the administrator's head. "He's turning into a merchant. Some bizarre variant of lycanthropy, no doubt.

"Hush," Kelly said, absorbing the giant's petulant expression without a flinch. "I'm bringing the line on. Ready?"

"Ready."

"*I've* been ready for seven minutes."

Kelly hovered over the intercom console. "Three, two, one, *live*."

Ghostly images of two men flickered into existence, in two of the three empty chairs at the table. The slender, dark one was Jorge Xavier. The other was a solidly-built Japanese whom Kelly recognized as Retsudo Oyama, the son of the founder of Oyama Construction.

"Gentlemen," Kelly said, using clear, careful diction. "Are you receiving us clearly?"

There was a perceptible delay before Retsudo answered her crisply. "Yes, thank you. Reception is fine. And you, Mr. Xavier?" His English sounded more British than American.

"Yes, thank you," Xavier said at once. "We had a problem with resolution, but it has been adjusted." He seemed somewhat stiff and unspontaneous. A handsome man, Kelly thought, but not an attractive one. "Please proceed."

"Gentlemen, Dr. Stonecypher, the head of the team which created the cable, is on my left. Mrs. Kelly is recording. Do we have any opening comments?"

Xavier cleared his throat. "I would like to point out that the sale of the cable should be influenced by other factors than sheer weight of gold."

"Indeed it has, Mr. Xavier," Stonecypher said with infinite gravity. "The fact that only two of you are left at this stage of the bidding indicates that quite clearly."

"Excuse me. I didn't mean the political pressures. It is possible that BTE can make an offer based upon a mutually profitable future relationship. We have Shuttle launch and refueling capabilities, which you may find useful in your present situation—"

"We have already made arrangements with the Japanese government, Mr. Xavier." A trace of annoyance thinned Fleming's lips. "You may rest assured that these arrangements will in no way affect today's bidding. The outcome will be based solely on the highest offer."

Oyama seemed curious. "Mr. Xavier, you speak as if you have already conceded defeat."

"Not at all. We are prepared to top your bid. I merely wished to point out that there are many ways that payment can be made, and that liquid assets are only one form."

"But what Falling Angel needs now are liquid assets," Fleming said quietly. "The item in question is already packaged for reentry, and can be available for shipping within ten hours. Shipping can be completed within five days, and will commence after the first third of the payment has been transferred to our bank in Zurich. We trust that this will be satisfactory. Dr. Stonecypher will accompany the cable personally to guarantee its safety."

Fleming looked from face to face. "Are there any further questions? No? Then let the bidding conclude."

A small white rectangle appeared in front of each holographic image, and hovered there. "You understand the rules, gentlemen. Each of you will be allowed one bid, and one bid only. The highest bid buys the cable." Tension had eased some of the depth from his voice, making it higher and thinner than usual. "May I have your bids, please?"

Xavier's rectangle filled at once:

$120,000,000

Fleming nodded approvingly. "Mr. Oyama, are you ready?" The Oriental could not see Xavier's bidding box, but still he gazed studiedly at Xavier. Xavier's remarks earlier: had that been trickery, to lull him into lowering his bid? If BTE topped Oyama by one dollar, the cable was theirs.

Oyama's rectangle filled with a nine-digit number:

$176,000,000

Retsudo was poised on the edge of his seat, as if ready to fly or fight. His hands were knotted painfully tight on the desk in front of him.

"Thank you, Mr. Oyama. Mr. Xavier, I'm afraid Oyama Construction has topped your bid."

Xavier made a little bow in his seat. "Congratulations, Mr. Oyama. Perhaps another time, Mr. Fleming." His image fuzzed out.

If a ton of steel girders had been lifted from Retsudo's chest, his relief could have been no greater. "Now, Mr. Fleming. I can assure you that the first payment will be deposited to your account within forty-eight hours. May I ask that the cable be ready for shipment as soon as you have received word . . .?"

The rest of the details—high finance and ground control—were relatively easy to workout, and within fifteen minutes Oyama had faded from the room. Fleming and Stonecypher grinned at each other with the unaffected pleasure of two children let loose in a toy store. "We did it." Fleming's voice was muted with wonder. "A hundred and seventy-six million dollars."

"Even inflation doesn't bite that too badly. Falling Angel has definitely hung out the shingle." Stonecypher ran skeletal fingers through his thinning shock of white hair. "We need to make decisions now, though. Our pilots are going to be busy ferrying the candy-pants back to *terra firma*. We'll need the very best pilots for the cable."

Fleming glanced at Kelly, who raised an eyebrow and silently mouthed a single syllable. Fleming nodded and turned back. "That would be Janet De Camp. Her husband Thomas would be my choice for ion drive tech. They're both space crazy—wouldn't think of going back."

"Yes, Thomas. Good man. We've traded pawns a few times. Isn't he prepping one of the ion drives for the Juno mining project?"

"Right, that's *Gabriel*, the one with the thermonuclear backup motor. He's been working on the others too. Nothing wrong with them, but he won't *be* here if anything *does* need repair. We were lucky there. The ion drive components came up before the political situation came apart. NASA could have stopped those flights."

Kelly was fidgetting uncomfortably. "Boss? This isn't anything official, but in a community this size it's hard not to pick up rumors."

Stonecypher clicked his puzzlement, leaning forward at the table. "This has some bearing on Thomas's fitness to accompany the cable?"

"It might affect his compatability profile. He and his wife are separating. Nothing hostile, just ... well, Dexter, you know Thomas. Introvert. Lives in his machines. He's never been much of a socializer."

Stonecypher's long frame stiffened slightly. "I've never heard of his having problems with anyone. We're here to work, not socialize. De Camp is a worker. I can understand that."

Kelly spread her hands helplessly. "I'm not passing judgement. I'm just trying to put my finger on the problem. What it boils down to is that his wife Janet started playing the field.

There are six men for every woman up here, and that's an awful temptation to a healthy girl."

"How serious is the rift?" Fleming asked.

"They're being very civil about it. But he's heading for the asteroids, and Janet is staying in the Earth-Moon system. Separation, for sure. I don't know about divorce."

"And your judgement?"

"Thomas puts his job first. Always. We can trust him. Janet's every bit as much the pro, she just knows how to cut loose, and he doesn't."

"All right. I think we can let Janet choose her own copilot from whoever's available. And that will round out the crew. What ship? Isn't *Anansi* due for repairs?"

"Yes, sir. Cargo bay doors need realignment. The other Shuttles are in Go condition, but *Haephestus* is still in Japan."

"O-Kay. Four Shuttles and only two cans, right? And the cans hold fifty-four passengers each. We can take our departures—"

"Deserters," Stonecypher corrected politely.

"—down in three loads. *Lucifer* and *Susanoo*, bring a can back and send *Haephestus*. *Anansi* goes with the cable pod. Tell Gomez that we want *Anansi* ready by the time Oyama's check clears."

"Yes sir. I'll get on it immediately." Kelly stood, in a smooth, graceful motion that took years to master. The trick was to thrust against Coriolis force *and* keep one's feet on the floor. She paused before leaving. "Sir?"

Fleming lifted a bushy gray eyebrow.

"I'm glad Oyama got the bid. There's something about that man Xavier that bothers me."

Her boss merely laughed quietly before turning back to Stonecypher.

Kelly left the room, still unable to dispell the disquieting image of the too-handsome man with the silver hair and the oily smile. *"Perhaps another time . . ."* Just a personal reaction, she decided. Very unprofessional of her.

Janet De Camp detached her helmet and took a deep breath as the airlock opened. It wasn't bottled air she hated, though she thought it was. All air was bottled air at Falling Angel, except in the greenhouse bubbles themselves. What ruined the taste of pressure suit air was being confined in that helmet.

She stripped down to a light green leotard, and hung her pressure suit on the rack near the inner door. There was one other suit on the rack.

She poised on the lip of the lock and took off, sailing into the air like a competition diver. She caught the first bar of the jungle gym and twisted her body lithely, working through it with practiced ease. The exercise room was another Shuttle tank, hauled up out of Earth's gravity well, fitted with an oxygen recycler and spun from one end. The gradient of weight return was sharp enough to provide a thorough and totally unique workout to those who used the monkey bars instead of the ladder which ran down the back wall.

Leg at full extension, she hooked her heel on a bar above her head and hoisted herself up with one leg, spun in a tight ball and caught another bar. Her performance would have been impossible under any but the weakest of gravities. She climbed and twisted "down" the bars, working against coriolis force and increasing spin-weight. She turned a horizontal bar into a side horse, doing a quick series of leg circles and then a backward scissors.

She was beginning to perspire now. She descended the rest of the way as if she were working parallel bars, swinging up, then dropping to the next level, hoisting herself into a handstand—and banging her ankle on another bar.

Janet's grip faltered, and she fell a few feet, catching herself frantically with a grip that would have shattered her wrist on Earth. Somewhat shamefaced, she lowered herself the rest of the way, the returning weight pressing the bars into her bare feet. The monkey bars, welded to the sides of the tank, ended eight feet above the floor, and she dropped, favoring the bruised ankle.

Lazy applause praised her efforts. "Bravo. Wonder Woman displays another of her myriad skills." The speaker was a slender blond man with finely chiseled muscles. His features were delicate enough to seem pretty, except for his nose, which was a trifle too large. He was stripped to the waist and glistened with the sweat of exertion. He shook his head violently, and an expanding halo of droplets flew from his hair.

"I'll make it all the way, Marion. You'll see." She limped over to him—an exaggerated limp, certainly—and watched as he slid back under the handles of the exercise machine. He pressed the handles up against two hundred pounds of air pressure and pumped it twice. It went halfway up the third time, then with a despairing *whoof!* he let it clatter back down.

Janet applauded sarcastically. "Bravo."

"I've been doing this for almost an hour, if you must know." He sat up, and wiped his face with his cotton T-shirt, gazing at her with narrowed eyes. "May I assume that you aren't here just for a workout?"

"I hear that you're leaving."

Marion swung one leg over the bench, sitting sideways, and mopped his chest with the shirt. "Is that question business or pleasure?"

"We need you, Marion."

His eyes were chips of green ice. "I never realized how impersonal a plural could be."

"Look. We're fighting for something you believe in. Don't try to tell that what happened between us changed your mind about Falling Angel."

He said nothing, but leaned away from her

a bare fraction.

She tried to smile. "Will you fly with me? Just this last time?"

"I really can't, Janet." His face softened, and he seemed even younger than his twenty-eight years. "I . . . have assets in American banks. A savings account, Uncle Gavin's trust fund—they could be frozen or attached. I can't afford to stay, and I can't afford to help you get that cable down." She watched him without speaking, and at last he shrugged, pulling his shirt on over his sweat-slick torso. It stuck on the dampness, and he had to tug it down. "I won't be surprised if you don't understand, okay?"

Without a backward glance, he headed toward the ladder.

"Marion," she called after him. He stopped, one hand on the bottom rung. "Would you do it if it were safe? *Would you do it if I weren't the pilot?*"

He rolled his shoulders under the pullover, turned to face her. "Maybe. Since it doesn't matter, maybe I would. Even if you were the pilot. But that's not the way things are, so why don't we cut the conversation, Janet?"

"I think we could swing it," she said carefully. She watched his eyebrows arch in disbelief, and hurried on. "Listen. We can list you as a deserter. One of the cargos of Earthbound can land in Japan a few days before us. You change places with their copilot once we've landed, and go back to America. They may suspect something, but not enough to stand up in court.''

Hope flared for a moment in his face, and her heart lifted. He *did* care about Falling Angel. He tucked his emotions back in as soon as he realised they were showing. "What if it doesn't work? I stand to lose quite a bit."

"That will be our department. You help us get this cable down, and if anything goes wrong you'll find yourself with a numbered Swiss account in the amount of your losses. Please, Marion. I wouldn't trust anyone else to be with me on this run. We . . . *I* need you."

There was the embryo of a smile tugging his thin lips into a bow. He shook his head ruefully. "Damn you, Janet. You've always got everything figured out, don't you?"

"All but one thing," she said. "I'm still not sure you're going to say 'yes.'"

He saw her smile waver for an instant, and knew her words were true. "All right," he said finally. "I've always had this thing about being needed."

Until he said those words, she hadn't realized that there was a tiny packet of constricted air in the base of her lungs. It went now, hot and stale, and she felt pounds lighter.

"Don't go gushy on me," he said without sarcasm. "I've got to pack, and this is no time for a scene." He turned and started up the ladder, whistling. He seemed lighter too, Janet noticed. Some people just need an ex-

cuse to do the things they wanted to do in the
first place.

Four

THE MAN WITH NO FRIENDS

The splintered brown expanse of the Elburz mountains fell away from under the BOAC jet as it made its approach to Mehrabad Airport. Djalma Costa buckled his seatbelt and pushed his body back into the seat, gripping his armrests with moist hands. The Industrial Relations laison of BTE had never enjoyed flying, had never trusted planes totally. The feeling of unease frequently blossomed into airsickness during the landing approach. Djalma could never eradicate the image of flames and twisted steel and mangled bodies, but he had learned to leech the color from them. Now his mind was filled with savage black and white arabesques of destruction: unnerving, but tolerable.

The Eurasian stewardess walked the aisle,

checking the passengers. She paused at his seat. "Please place your briefcase under the seat in front of you, unless you'd like me to—"

He nodded with nervous quickness. He slid the black case gingerly under the seat, then placed his right foot atop the case, so that it took only a slight pressure to reassure himself that it was still there. He closed his eyes and breathed slowly, concentrating on the fact that within minutes he would be in Teheran.

Costa's contact met him as soon as he had passed through customs. "Welcome to Iran," the man said politely, making a shallow bow. "Mr. Hoveida sent me."

Costa nodded, only the barest spark of suspicion still alive in his mind. "And who is Mr. Hoveida's friend?"

The man's light brown face crinkled into a knowing smile. "Mr. Hoveida has no friends, sir. His partner, however, is Mr. Reza Mansur."

Costa nodded. "All right. Take my bags. I'll carry the briefcase."

The waiting car was a battered Chevrolet station wagon. Inconspicuous. Good. He slid into the front seat and waited for the driver to finish stowing the luggage. They moved out into traffic, and Costa closed his eyes, running through a mental file on Hoveida.

Born 1968 in Ma'ad, Jordan, he had attended the University of Amman and be-

come involved in radical politics. He first
came to the attention of Interpol in '87 as the
result of a PLO bombing raid on an Israeli
synagogue. He went underground soon afterward, surfacing in Afghanistan as an arms
dealer, in Baghdad as a hired gun, and once in
Paris, soliciting financial support for a new
organization, the United Moslim Activist
Front. Claiming to represent the interests of
all Arabs, he gained backing from several
sources—some said that Middle Eastern
OPEC interests were heavily involved—and
was suspected to have been behind some of
the most audacious acts of terrorism of the
1990's.

It was known that he had acquired a critical
mass of plutonium, with plans to blackmail a
western nation, most probably the United
States. Word had leaked, and the enforcement
arm of the United Nations Nuclear Limita-
tions committee descended on his headquar-
ters in Edmonton, Alberta. Spearheaded by
the RCMP, the operation had been a complete
success—the plutonium recovered, the
terrorist organization smashed. Only Hoveida
had escaped.

Hoveida knew that one of three people had
betrayed him. All three of them were close
friends of his. Unable to determine which of
them was the traitor, he had taken the only
expedient course of action, killing all three.

Since that time, Hassan Ali Hoveida had
been known as "The man with no friends."

Here, in Iran, Hoveida had found a new home for the United Moslim Activist Front. Officially denounced and outlawed by the Iranian Parliament, they had nonetheless operated out of Teheran for the past six years with a minimum of difficulty. Costa feared notice by American and Soviet agents more than any Iranian security forces.

Djalma was jarred from his musing by a jolt as the station wagon pulled up to the curb. They were in front of a fairly modern two-story dwelling, by its weathering perhaps ten years old. It clearly showed the influence of Westernization on Iranian culture, being barely distinguishable from any suburban house in America.

He waited for the chauffeur to remove the bags from the back, then followed him to the house. There was a five-second pause after a rhythmic knock, and the door opened. He was led down a narrow wood-paneled hall decorated with hanging rugs and lit with a single dull bulb. It jarred with the modern exterior: perhaps a misguided attempt to capture a bygone simplicity.

The hallway opened into a circular room where a plain wooden table sat, holding an electric lamp. There were three men in the room. He recognized Mansur by his cadaverous thinness and precisely groomed beard. Mansur sat at the table, using a crust of bread to sop the last drops of gravy from a plate. Behind him stood a huge man with a discernable lump beneath his light coat. Bodyguard.

The third man sat at the table, paring an apple very precisely with a folding knife. He was light for a Jordanian, and his face was a calm oval. His shoulders were broad but slack, relaxed almost lethargically. Costa had met him twice before, and both times had been stricken by the lack of warmth in the room. Regardless of the temperature else-where in the house, Hoveida's presence was always like a draft of cold air.

"Sit down, please." Hoveida's English was heavily accented, a strong element of French mixed with the Arabic.

Djalma sat, laying out his briefcase and crossing his legs carefully. "I am prepared to offer you a half million Pounds Sterling for your organization's participation in this venture."

Hoveida nodded soberly. "As agreed. I be-lieve that our combined resources can ac-complish this thing."

"The money will buy much ammunition, many guns and bribes. There is no problem with manpower?"

"None. It is, after all, a holy cause." A flicker of grim amusement curled Hoveida's mouth in a smile.

"So long as the equipment arrives on schedule," Mansur said quietly, "there should be no problem with the firing."

A wedge of apple vanished into Hoveida's

mouth, and he chewed thoughtfully. "Of course, it is good that the men understand that this spaceship of yours does indeed threaten us. If they didn't understand this thing, it might seem as if the money were a primary motivation." Djalma glanced at the bodyguard, a huge dark man with hollow eyes. The man was too tense.

"Let me explain again," Djalma said, taking the hint smoothly. "The developing nations of the world have always been stripped of their resources by the industrial nations. Many of us have based our economy chiefly on the exportation of materials and energy, and through great struggles, have forced the robber nations to pay us a fair price for our goods. Now they prepare to rape the asteroid belt, and a network of solar power satellites is under construction, which will soon ring the earth.

"Perhaps the two best forms of storing solar energy are, one, using it to dissociate water into hydrogen and oxygen. The hydrogen can be liquified and used as fuel. Two, use solar power to make methyl alcohol from water and air and garbage. Either method reduces the dependency of the industrial nations on petroleum products, weakening the economy of any oil producing country, particularly in the Middle East.

"It is time to show America, Russia, and Japan that they cannot despoil the Earth, then escape to the stars. They must be shown their vulnerability as graphically as possible. The spacecraft of Falling Angel Enterprises provide an ideal target. Due to the present dispute between Falling Angel and America's National Aeronautics and Space Administration, Falling Angel has declared its independence."

Costa grinned wolfishly. "This means that they are no longer under the direct protection of the United States. We can attack them and America will shake her head and say: 'Isn't it terrible, the things that can happen to wayward children? Come back to the fold, and we will protect you.' Now is the time to strike, gentlemen."

Hoveida nodded, watching Mansur out of the corner of his eye. After devouring another slice of apple, he turned to the thin man. "I am satisfied with the money and the justification. The men will do as I say. The rest is your end, Mansur. It would be best to ask any basic questions now."

Costa had the distinct feeling that Mansur did not like him, or trust him. It was in the slow turning of the head, the moistening of narrow lips with a brownish tongue. It mattered little. The man was a weapons and explosives expert, perhaps the finest who had ever gone "Underground" in the Middle East. He had been responsible for the design of the plutonium device captured in Edmonton. Experts had determined that the hellish thing, briefcase-sized, could have done more damage than the one detonated over Nagasaki in 1945.

"I do not doubt," Mansur began, his accent so thick that Costa had difficulty distinguishing the consonants, "that you can obtain a Prometheus missile. The resources of Brazil Techimetal and Electromotores are well known."

In shock, Costa looked to Hoveida, and to the guard who stood quietly against the wall. Hoveida laughed harshly. "No, little man. I didn't give your secret away."

"But then how—? No one was supposed to know—"

"I am not ignorant of international business affairs, Mr. Costa. I am well aware of BTE's recent bid for Falling Angel's products. Your bid failed. I can understand vengeance quite well." Mansur's head bobbed on his pipestem neck like a puppet on a string, and his colorless eyes shone with pleasure. "Did you really think that I would involve myself in a project of this kind without knowing all of the details? Vengeance against Falling Angel. And what would Oyama Construction call your actions? Preemptive competition?" His body shook as he laughed.

"Very well." Costa mopped his forehead. "But I trust that this information will go no further?"

"Certainly. As I was saying before you became so upset, I have no doubt that you can obtain a ground-to-orbit missile. I need to know how you plan to deliver it to our launch site."

The smile on Costa's face was an uneasy thing, held by force of will alone. He riffled through his briefcase until he found the papers he needed, and laid them out on the table. "Now," he began, breath rasping in his throat. "The Prometheus missile will be brought in by tanker through the Persian Gulf to Bandar-e-Shahpur. It will be contained in twenty-three boxes labeled 'machine parts.' The necessary officials have already been bribed or—" He glanced at Hoveida, who, expressionless, was slipping the last section of apple into his mouth. "—removed."

He skipped to another sheet of paper, reading down a quarter of a page before continuing. "From there, it will be shipped by rail, north to Qom, and from there Southeast to Ardestan. Then we will need trucks to relay the boxes to the launch site. You have kept the exact coordinates of the site a secret, although we know it is in the desert near Isfahan."

Hoveida had stopped moving, was totally motionless, and again Costa had the feeling that the room temperature had dropped. "That is all you need to know. It is actually more than you need to know."

Mansur broke the icy silence. "Your communications and telemetry personnel will be accompanying the missile?"

"No, only the missile crew will actually

accompany it. The rest will come in by helicopter from Kuwait."

Mansur and Hoveida spoke for a minute in Arabic, then Mansur rose and left the room, his bodyguard following silently.

Hoveida grinned broadly, exposing a split tooth in the back of his mouth. "Come. We must make you at home. After all, you are to be our guest for the next several days. There is much work to do, and it will be good for you to rest."

"Yes. I didn't get any coming in from Moscow."

"Yes. The Russians. They did not open your briefcase? Good." Hoveida stretched, yawning, then snapped his head around as if a thought had just occurred to him. "I think that you had better give me the money now. It will be much safer, don't you think?"

"Of course." Costa peeled off a false lining in his briefcase and stripped out six short stacks of paper. He riffled through them, then placed the stack on the table in front of Hoveida. "Count it."

"I am sure there is no need. We understand each other all too well. Please, go now. Rest yourself." He waved an arm expansively. "I am sure you will find the accomodations to your liking. Rest. There is much work to be done tomorrow."

Costa clicked his case shut and rose. "Well, then. I will see you later this evening."

"No. Tomorrow."

"Tomorrow." He bowed slightly and took his leave, noticing that the temperature seemed to rise as he left Hoveida's presence. He was sweating, but he didn't think that his hands were trembling too badly. He was playing a deadly game here, deadly. Mansur thought that the United Moslim Activist Front had "all of the details."

They didn't. They didn't know about the helicopter which would carry Costa to safety at the proper moment. They didn't know about BTE's plan for the cable.

They didn't understand the true role of the Prometheus missile. *Window dressing!*

He had to be very careful. So much depended upon nuances and proper timing. Costa trudged up the staircase, clutching his briefcase tightly, feeling a headache coming on. Death, and unimaginable riches, were hovering in the air about him. He wondered which would come to roost first.

Five

THE PRESSURE COOKER

Falling Angel emerged from the shadow of the Moon, and glaring sunlight swept across the clusters of cylinders. It picked up the Cable Assembly like a spotlight. Marion Guiness, sucking gravy from his fingers in the commissary, barked startled laughter.

He covered his mouth with his hand and peered around guiltily. Nobody seemed to have noticed. *How did I miss that yesterday?* he wondered. *It's grotesque. It looks like some kids tried to make a pickaxe out of old spacecraft models.*

The space shuttle *Anansi* formed the blunt-beaked blade of the pickaxe. The haft was two components: the ion drive tug, *Gabriel*, and the re-entry pod sandwiched between.

The re-entry pod housed the Stonecypher

Cable. Designed for one use only, it looked like a long, flat-bellied boulder with fins embedded in the tail. The hull and fins were covered with handholds. Ten small solid rocket motors—limpet motors—were mounted around the tail. Prongs anchored in its nose were moored to *Anansi*'s belly, in the support points where an external tank would ride during a Shuttle's ascent into orbit.

The ion drive floated behind the cable pod, not yet docked, shaping the rest of the pickaxe handle. *Gabriel* looked like a steel brick with lumps on it.

The dustless vacuum robbed the Cable Assembly of all sense of scale. Marion knew its size. He had worked twelve hours yesterday in *Anansi*'s cargo bay. Though new to Falling Angel, the Shuttle had served NASA for fourteen years. Wide areas of kitchen-tile heat shielding had worn thin enough to need replacing, and the rest was examined before every flight into Earth's lethal atmosphere. Payload was light this trip, mostly widgetry for handling the cable; but if those masses started bouncing around during re-entry . . .

Anansi alone was huge. The cable pod was almost as big, and equally massive. *Gabriel* was smaller by a third. But there was no blurring to show the size of that crude pickaxe. It might well have been toy-sized, until the eye found other cues.

There: tiny human forms, pudgy in pressure suits, swarming around *Anansi*. The cargo bay doors flapped like slow wings, opening, closing, testing the repaired hinge systems. She was a lovely beast. At thirty-seven meters, she and her sister Shuttles were the largest self-propelled objects in the Earth-Moon system.

Marion remembered the thrill of surfing a flaming shock wave through Earth's upper atmosphere, and fought an urge to shiver. One more flight . . .

Pressure-suited men and women surrounded *Gabriel*, too, readying it for its maiden flight. It bothered Marion to know that one of the men working on *Gabriel* was Janet's husband.

He didn't wonder why she hadn't told him *that*. She'd needed his promise first. He wasn't even particularly angry. That was just . . . Janet. But it was something that ought to be settled soon.

Marion finished his coffee, dumped his tray and was on his way to the airlock.

Lines still moored *Anansi* to the hangar and storage cylinders. Marion crossed by one of these, pushing his pressure-duffle ahead of him, letting its mass tow him. He entered via the airlock in the cargo bay. The pressure suit was uncomfortably tight now, but he left it on while he climbed to the cockpit.

Janet was already there, but busy. She nodded perfunctorily before returning to her checkout. She played her hands over the instruments like a master pianist caressing the keyboard. He knew that blank look. Only her body occupied the command chair; her mind was in the miles of wire and tubing, re-establishing an almost symbiotic link with *Anansi*. He had spent hundreds of hours in the cockpit with her, and knew that her flying was less an intellectual appreciation of readout than a kind of kinesthetic perception whereby she became one with her craft: its engines her muscles, its thermal-insulated aluminum sheathing her skin.

He went back down to the airlock. The pump whirred down to silence; his pressure suit lost its tightness.

The cargo bay doors had been left open. Marion coasted down the vast empty space. His gaze picked out bulges in the sprayed foam-plastic padding that covered the floor and walls. Cargo crates, some pressurized, all protected against a turbulent re-entry. Above him, the foam-titanium roof curved away in a great arc. He moored a safety line at the back wall, then used mobility pack jets to go over the side.

The cable package was locked beneath *Anansi*'s tiled belly. Those prongs, like the handholds, like the mating ring at the cable pod's tail, were only lunar pig iron; they would melt away during re-entry. Marion sailed along the length of the cable pod and across the gap to *Gabriel*.

Marion knew something about space

propulsion systems—ion drives, solar sails, linear accelerators—enough to hold his own in a conversation, and no more. Those things didn't fly. They pushed, or fell, or sailed; but since his earliest school days the thing that had fascinated Marion Guiness was flight. When other children were torn between wanting to be policemen or baseball players, Marion watched the skies. When boys his age were thinking of proms and driver's licenses, Marion was an Honors student at the Air Force flight academy. Be it hang gliding, or riding a supersonic shock wave across the sky in a combination meteor/surfboard/winged metal building, or anything in between, he loved it. Life in free fall didn't bother him as long as he exercised, and Falling Angel gave him the chance to fly occasionally.

He found Thomas De Camp in the ion drive's tiny cockpit. It was open, and De Camp was in full pressure suit, taking readings from one of the computer screens. He dictated into his suit mike while liquid-crystal readouts flashed before him. Marion scanned his helmet radio band to find Thomas's frequency.

"Hey there, Tom. What's the problem?" He winced at the somewhat forced jollity in his voice.

De Camp looked up and spotted Guiness, and bent back down to his work. "Just a minute."

Marion waited, worrying. He and the half-

Eskimo tech had never been good friends, but there had never been animosity either. Many of the married men in space had had to face the fact of infidelity so rampant that it transcended the abnormal. But "many men" reacted as points on a graph. How Thomas De Camp, cuckold, would react to being shut up for a week with his wife and his wife's ex-lover, was another topic altogether.

De Camp pushed himself up out of the cockpit, braked with a tug on his safety line. "Hello, Marion." The voice coming over the receiver was flat with tension.

That might be for personal reasons, or professional. Marion gambled on professional. "Is there a problem?"

His father's dark skin, his mother's fat-padded face, made Thomas resemble a sooty Buddha when he pouted. "Wouldn't be a problem if I had the extra month I was supposed to have."

"Hell, you were on your way to the asteroids! I'd think a shakedown is a good idea. If there's trouble on the way to Earth, we're still close enough to yell for help."

Thomas was shaking his head. "If there's trouble, then I fluffed it. If I fluff it, it's because they short-changed me by a month! This is my job, and I should have a chance to do it right." His eyes narrowed. "I would think you'd understand that."

Marion broke eye contact, clearing his throat. He eyed the steel-and-glass bubble moored to the ion drive assembly. It wasn't small, but food and water and oxygen storage and instrumentation panels left little room for a man. "I'd want a cockpit that was bigger than this."

"Think of it as a small igloo," Thomas said, turning back to his work. "It'll be enlarged before *Gabriel* goes out to the asteroids. Anyway, I've got more room than the old *Mercury* capsules."

"You'll be *four days* coming back to the Moon."

"I'll be all right."

The sentence was tantamount to a dismissal. Marion listened to the sound of his own breathing in his helmet, then tried again. "Tom . . .?"

The ion drive tech turned back, irritation showing. "Yes?"

"We're going to be spending the next week together . . . I just thought you should know that it's over between Janet and me."

"Congratulations."

Marion felt himself bristle. "How do you mean that?"

"I could be wrong, but I'd think you had too much intelligence to be one of her trinkets. Oh, you're pretty enough, but you don't *seem* to be an inverterbrate." He laughed harshly, without looking up. "Anyway, I'm glad you directed her to the playground down the street."

"You're pretty dry about all this."

Another laugh. "What am I supposed to do, jump and scream? We're about through with each other, anyway. After this trip, it's me for Juno, and Janet can do what she pleases."

"No divorce?"

"If she wants to file papers, I'll be glad to sign. Looking at the way things turned out, that's not too likely, though, is it?"

"I don't understand you."

"You're not required to." He turned back to his work. "Now, if you'll excuse me, we're about ready to mate this thing to the cable pod. You'd better get yourself clear."

He released his safety line and jumped toward the looming belly of *Anansi*, sparing his backpack fuel. Marion watched him for a few seconds, then called after him. "Thomas —I loved her."

De Camp's voice came back. "Did it make a difference?"

"I don't think she ever believed it."

"She will now. This is an open frequency."

Marion swore and looked down at his chin display. It . . . wasn't an open frequency. He heard De Camp's chuckle cut off as he passed behind the Shuttle bay doors.

Dexter Stonecypher's office was roughly spherical. A videobeam projector illuminated a third of the curving white inner shell. At the moment the beam was split into ten separate images. Dominating the center was a view of *Gabriel*, a huge steel brick closing massively on the mating ring at the stern of the cable pod. Surrounding that image were nine smaller views, giving alternate angles on the pod, technical readouts, and video feeds from his Special Projects division.

From a couch webbing set flush against the opposing wall, Stonecypher watched the progress on the center screen while he sucked coffee from a squeezebottle. His eyes were red and his hand trembled. Thirty hours without sleep had nearly laid him low. He trusted his subordinates, but the cable was his child, his concept, his creation. To allow anyone else to oversee its journey to Earth would have been dereliction of duty.

He spoke softly: "Command swap Four for One." The central image traded places with one of the smaller screens. He was looking over the pod now, watching the approach of the ion drive. The cable, over twenty tons of it, was coiled on an immense reel and sheltered within a steel housing. The housing was cased thickly in foamed lunar slag, forming a shape halfway between an airplane and a boulder: flattened at the belly, rounded at the nose, with three hatchet-blade fins and the motors to turn them mounted at the tail. Despite its makeshift look, it was aerodynamically sound. He'd worked on the computer animated re-entry test. Major restructuring of the exterior housing had been necessary ... though that was no problem; it only involved adding more of the lunar rock.

Mountains of raw material were available from the lunar surface, and hemispherical mirrors provided the heat to turn ore into pure metal and alloy. Indeed, Falling Angel made alloys that would have been impossible on Earth. A gravitational field can cause materials of varying densities to "layer up" like a *pousse-cafe*. That doesn't happen in free fall . . . and neither does heat convection; that had been a serious problem, once. It had been solved. Falling Angel's zero-gravity labs had made possible the gallium bismide semiconductors which had revolutionized the home electronics field.

But that was in the dead past, and right now Stonecypher's near-weightless body felt heavy with fatigue. He was alone in his office, his door *Do Not Disturb*ed to stop his assistants from reminding him to go to bed. He sat with knees drawn up, strapped into his vertical couching, and blinked slowly as one of the peripheral screens blinked rapidly, demanding his attention.

"Biolab." The small screen blossomed into center position. A pressure-suited technician faced the camera, holding a polyethylene bag filled with red-blotched gray fur balls.

Oh, yes, Dexter thought wearily. The rats. Every experiment that didn't fall under an established heading came under the scope of Special Projects, including Project Plague.

When *Pasteurella pestis* confines itself to an infection cycle of rat-flea-rat, it is untroublesome to man. When the disease kills off so many of the rat population that the fleas cannot find proper hosts, they will accept human beings instead. But in general it spreads from man to man only with the cooperation of migrating fleas. When the disease becomes pneumonic, attacking the lungs, infesting phlegm and saliva with virulent bacteria, plague becomes most fearsome, spreading directly from human to human, leaving death in its path.

Pasteurella pestis is extinct, of course. One with the dead—

In Jamshedpur, eastern India, a bulldozer had torn up several unmarked, makeshift graves. The Black Death lived again.

Isolated from Earth, possessed of a unique environment for the preparation of plague vaccine, Falling Angel had accepted the challenge. Rats, fleas, and infected human blood and tissue had been shuttled out to lunar orbit. Rats in the hundreds had sickened and been studied, dissected, re-infected, allowed to die. Plague was extracted from blood solutions with electric fields. The process, electrophoresis, couldn't be used in a gravity field because the heat caused convection within the fluid medium, contaminating or destroying the biological materials.

Falling Angel offered another advantage, the results of which Stonecypher watched with ill-disguised irritation. "Dr. Quinn. It seems that you've captured the errant rodents."

Quinn shook the plastic bag. The freeze-dried puffballs rattled like so many hard meringues. "What's left of them, yes."

"And the *Xenopsylla astia?*" The face on the screen went blank for a moment, and Dexter leapt into the breech. "The fleas, dammit man. I want each and every carapaced corpse ennumerated and accounted for." Behind Dr. Quinn other workers in pressure suits ran magnifying viewers along the corners and crevices, inspecting the rows of anchored glass tubes and hooded flasks. Equipment was being dismantled and removed from the room for further disinfection. "After diverting my funds, personnel and administrative time for the past fourteen hours, I should like to hear that something positive has come of our little excitement."

"Dr. Stonecypher, we're doing the best we can," Quinn said apologetically. "We're just glad we could contain the problem by depressurizing the section." He tried a grin. "Can you imagine the results if this happened at the Mayo Clinic?"

"There shouldn't have *been* a problem."

"Now, Doctor. You've had your own problems with contaminants, ruptured lines—"

"True enough, young man. But the plastics and metals I work with don't actively attempt to chew through rubber flanges. If they did, I would be somewhat more attentive than you seem to have been."

"Doctor . . ."

"I have no more time. Proceed, please, or must I come down there with a whiskbroom and a pan to help?"

Quinn shook his head uneasily and broke the contact. Dexter rubbed his eyes and had the momentary good sense to check his pulse, forefinger gently pressing the vein in his wrist. His heart was racing, near 120. Fatigue, he told himself. Stress. The coffee. Or . . .

But that was unthinkable. Not now, not when he was needed so badly. His cable would buy freedom for Falling Angel, and nothing else mattered. He had taken three years of his life to design it, and two to set up the facility. Adding two more for the actual extrusion process, and the damned cable had stolen seven years of his life. Perhaps he was becoming a little obsessive about the project, but who wouldn't be?

Again he fingered his wrist, searching for the pulse. He felt it flutter, and sucked air. If he wasn't careful, very careful . . .

Despite the *Do Not Disturb* on his door, he heard a hesitant knock, then a swish as it opened.

Stonecypher stretched his long frame, forcing crispness into the motion. A familiar profile blotted out the videobeam. "Mrs. Kelly," he said wearily as she swung herself up onto the webbing. "Have you lost the ability to read? The sign is most explicit."

"Dr. Stonecypher—"

"I don't want to hear it. I am extremely busy right now—"

Lips pursed, Kelly studied Dexter's face. She didn't like what she saw. "You're too tired. Fleming is worried about you—"

"He is, is he? Well you just march right back to Fleming and tell him that I can jolly well take care of—" He lunged forward, eyes fixed on one of the smaller screens. "Command swap Six for One." It flashed onto the darkened center screen, and he snatched at his throat mike. "This is Stonecypher. Are you monitoring this, Strickland? *Gabriel*'s picked up some angular momentum, and it's still moving. You'll mess up the cable pod unless you chill that right *now*."

Strickland's voice crackled over the speakers. "Got you, Doc, we've already caught it. Correction was started twenty seconds ago. See?"

Stonecypher leaned closer. "Computer animation," he said distinctly, and a blue rotating skeleton popped onto the right corner screen. He checked the numbers. "Right. Sorry to bother you."

"No problem, Doc."

Stonecypher sighed hugely, waved a shaking hand at the multiple screens. "Do you see? You see what I have to worry about? By gosh, woman, who do you think is going to do the work around here?"

"It seems to me that Strickland was doing just fine."

"Hmm. Yes. For the moment. Tell that to Quinn. I *can't* relax now. Do you think I *like* being in a pressure cooker?" Kelly seemed to be considering the question, and Stonecypher reacted with rage. "If Fleming ever stops cutting corners and gets some competent help up here, maybe then I'll believe that I can turn my back without the whole show going straight to hell!"

He was almost screaming now, and she could see how his hands were shaking. There was a light sheen of perspiration on his forehead, and Kelly bet herself that it was sticky and cool. She said, "Doctor, you have only seven hours before the cable is due to leave. They have to make their delivery deadline. You need your rest."

"The hell I do!" The side of his fist slammed down on his desk. He scraped a little skin off his knuckle, and his body jerked up against his couching in weightless reaction.

"All right, Doctor, I'll leave. But I'm going to turn off your terminal."

Stonecypher's heavy eyebrows nearly shot through the ceiling. "What?"

"We're not going to let you kill yourself on this project. If you want to commit suicide, swallow a tube of silicone patch." She turned like a wraith and glided through the door, pausing a moment to hear Dexter's inevitable sigh of defeat.

"Damn you, woman, you don't fight fair."

"I'm not playing for points, Doctor." And

she was gone.

Stonecypher turned back to his screen. It was all over. The ion drive was firmly mated to the rear of the cable pod. Now two cylinders alongside the steel brick began to unroll themselves.

He watched until the solar power collectors stood out from *Gabriel* like a pair of long rectangular wings. A moment later the screen went dead. Kelly's promise had been mercifully delayed, but not forgotten. He looked out his window, seeing the same approximate view, but without the close-up detail.

Stonecypher sighed and reached out a pipestem arm for the blanket tucked folded on one of his horizontal shelves. *Thank God for Kelly.* Sometimes he felt like an old machine whose automatic shutoff had frozen years back. He would just run on and on, until something broke or someone pulled his plug.

One day he would have to let Kelly know how much he appreciated her. Not soon, but someday.

He tucked the blanket around him and fastened two Velcro straps, turning the couch into a "sleepweb." "Command lights out," he said, and faded into fitful sleep.

Six

EARTHBOUND

There were four seats on the command level of *Anansi*: three standard, and one stretched-out monstrosity to handle the stretched-out frame of Falling Angel's chief metallurgist. Thomas patted the older man's shoulder as he edged past. "Good to have you along," he said.

Stonecypher nodded, still relaxed from his nap. "I assume you brought your board?"

Thomas nodded vigorously, buckling himself into his own seat, behind Janet. "You bet. And we've got a chess program in the on-board, so take your pick." He leaned forward to speak to his wife. "We weren't getting enough efficiency from the atomic plant."

"Everything's fine now, Tommy. Check the monitor." Janet leaned left in the command chair so that her husband could peek over her shoulder. Ahead of her, out the front window, there was nothing but pinpoint stars and, low in her horizon, a blue-white half-disk Earth. She could feel the adrenalin beginning to flow, as it always did before a mission, regardless of its size or importance. Joining with her craft, becoming part of the most advanced piece of flying machinery ever created by man, was an excitement beyond anything else in her life.

She glanced from Thomas to Marion and back again. Marion didn't feel that way about his work. And Thomas did! *Why can't I forgive him that?*

Thomas leaned forward and checked her readout. He matched it with figures in his mind, and nodded. "Good enough. We'll use the fission plant for departure, then damp it. Sunpower's free."

"*Anansi*, this is Falling Angel," the intercom hissed. "You have completed all test sequences, and everything here is Go. Comments?"

"Captain De Camp." She adjusted the sound level on her mike. "Everything in order here. Go." She glanced back at Stonecypher. He looked to be half asleep, but his straps were in place. Professional paranoia . . .

Fuel tanks, a swiveled motor, and an electromagnetic plate: that was a limpet motor. It weighed as much as a man and was half a man's size, and it was generally handled manually. It was relatively cheap, and very useful in free fall. Whatever you wanted moved, enough limpet motors would move it. There were twenty now on *Gabriel*. Ten more on the cable pod would drop it from Earth orbit to Japan.

A score of limpets fired, and the Cable Assembly moved away from Falling Angel. After a minute or so their carefully measured fuel ran out, not all at once; and as they did, the magnets cut off. The Cable Assembly left a trail of limpet motors behind itself, all joined by a hundred meters of safety cord. The last to go was a sled bearing two limpet motors and a man.

They watched the sled heading back, trailing dead limpet motors.

"We picked up a touch of spin," Janet said disapprovingly, and she keyed attitude jets. Her crew's bellies rolled with the peculiar motion. When it stopped, the Cable Assembly's pickaxe handle was parallel to the lunar surface, and Falling Angel had grown small enough to be cupped in two hands.

"Ion drive in ten," Thomas said. "Janet?"

"Fine."

"*Anansi*, this is Falling Angel. We monitor all systems as Go. Have a good trip. Check back when you round the Moon."

Cesium vapor flowed into *Gabriel*'s motor system. Positively charged grids stripped electrons from the cesium atoms, then sent them fleeing away, plus-charges repelling each other. *Anansi* accelerated with imperceptible gentleness on a breath of cesium-ion breeze.

Its path wound out from the Moon; became an expanding spiral. Falling Angel monitored through relays. At the end of six hours Falling Angel had become invisibly small below them, the Moon had become a good deal smaller, and their orbit was cometary. If the ion motor failed now, the Cable Assembly would not return to lunar orbit. Its target was Earth.

"Bishop to Queen's Knight three," Thomas said. Stonecypher watched him move the magnetic piece, and a smile tugged at the corners of his mouth.

Stonecypher castled.

The next move was pivotal, and Thomas relaxed a moment to think; but he found his thoughts drifting along other lines. It was easy to lose himself in abstractions once the mission was underway. Easy to begin a good game of chess with a friend, or to watch the pinpoint stars, or the hazy blue disk of Earth. His co-workers, the game, the myriad calculations and adjustments forever coalescing in the back of his mind, his memories of Alaska, would all blend into a single complete pattern, a tapestry of contented thought which was as close to poetry as he ever allowed himself to come.

Thoughts of Alaska were particularly close now, as he hovered over a game board in the forward compartment. In a week he would be in orbit around Earth, the closest he had been for months. He alone would not land. He would return to lunar orbit in that tiny cabin aboard the ion drive, and from there head out to Juno, a hundred and fifty million miles from Earth. How long would he stay? As long as he was needed. As long as there was work to absorb him, to help him forget the cold, crisp Alaskan mornings when it seemed that distance had no meaning, that faroff mountains, crisp and sharp in his vision, were near enough to reach out and touch.

To help the memory of Janet die away . . .or at least lose its sharp cutting edges. He frowned, and concentrated on the board in front of him.

"Who's hungry?" Marion said from the top of the ladder.

Thomas heard Janet's musical laugh, pictured her slipping off her headset and stretching, cool blue eyes alive with pleasure. "I feel like I haven't eaten for a week," she said.

"Good enough." Marion started down the ladder. "I'll see what's in the food locker." He saw Thomas and Stonecypher absorbed in their game, cocked his head sideways to get a better look at the board. "Pretty quiet down here. Who's slaughtering whom?"

"We'll know in a move or two. Meanwhile, hush."

Marion raised a blond eyebrow. "I hope Tom beats your pants off. Then I think I'll take a crack at it."

The metallurgist *tsk'd*. "No respect for

age." He studied the board, then looked up. "I am getting a bit itchy. Almost time to check on the cable."

Marion produced plastic envelopes filled with club sandwiches and Hershey bars. "Food?" Stonecypher smiled, Thomas nodded without looking up from the board. The copilot dropped off an envelope apiece and a pouch of cold milk, then climbed up the ladder to the flight deck.

After he was gone Thomas made his move.

Stonecypher watched his opponent place the piece, and chuckled. "You don't like him very much, do you?"

The small man chewed a hole in his plastic pouch and ripped it open. "It's your move." His eyes flickered up to the flight deck. He heard Marion laugh, and the barest trace of a grimace kissed his lips.

"Normally I wouldn't worry about you, Thomas," Stonecypher said, fingers brushing the ivory tip of a knight's mane. "But you're going to indulge an old man's nosiness— you're not letting it get to you, are you?"

Thomas's forehead creased in parallel rows. "Why do you ask?"

"Because you aren't thinking, youngster." He moved his knight. "Mate in three, I think."

Thomas savaged a great hunk from his sandwich, eyeing the board with his irritation giving way to humor. "Your game," he said, "and your point, too. I'll try to keep a lid on it."

Stonecypher nodded, tore open his own
package and started to eat. He barely nibbled
at his meal. Fatigue syruped his movements,
making them clumsy, making a lie of the light-
ness in his voice. Thomas started to speak, to
give warning, but he knew that part of that
urge was the wish to give Stonecypher a taste
of his own medicine. Unfair. The only thing
that would relax Falling Angel's elder statesman was an opportunity to do something useful: a mental state Thomas understood perfectly.

When Stonecypher pushed the remains of
his sandwich aside, and the plasticware was
gathered for the dishwasher, Thomas unhooked himself from his seat. "Let me stow
this," he said. "Then we can get some work
done."

The thin face nodded. "Yes, it's time to
check our cargo."

There was little sound, even from footsteps,
as they moved to the back of the lower deck,
shuffling carefully down a strip of Velcro
flooring. Surrounding them were lockers and
a good deal of working space, including plugs
and attachments and mountings for instru-
ment boards. In the rear was mounted the
elaborate control board Thomas used to
monitor and steer the ion drive. Next to it,
equally elaborate, the flight controls that
would guide the cable pod down through
Earth's atmosphere. Neither was equipped
with chairs; just handholds and more Velcro

rug.

Stonecypher glided to the cable pod controls, moving his preying-mantis frame with eery grace. "Let's have a look." His hands played over the console. Color video images sprang to life: a not very interesting view of *Anansi*'s tiled belly, another of the ion drive haloed in the faint violet glow of its exhaust, both relayed from a camera on the pod's vertical fin. Stonecypher must have found the cryptic streams of numbers on other screens more interesting, but still he relaxed noticeably.

"The pod's riding well," he said. "No vibration. No heat buildup."

"Good." But Thomas was watching Stonecypher's thickly veined hands, noting the tremble. He weighed his motivations, found them pure. "Dexter . . . you're not well, are you?"

Stonecypher blew through his lips, a sound of disgust. "When you get to be my age, it's a rare day when some part or other isn't acting up." He turned back to his work, a shade too quickly.

"I'm not talking generally. I've been watching you. Your hands shake, you have no appetite, your face is drawn. Were you checked out at Falling Angel?"

Stonecypher looked down from his towering height, imperiously or something like it. "Just what are you talking about?"

"I'm asking you if you have any business going down into Earth's gravity well. You'll have to take three gees to get out again, and I'm beginning to doubt you can take that safely."

A gnarled hand rubbed across a forehead that was suddenly damp with perspiration. He started to frame a sharper response, then sighed in defeat. "All right. All right, Thomas, I'm not well. Perhaps I shouldn't make this trip—" He waved off De Camp's attempt to interject a word. "Perhaps I shouldn't—if all I care about is my own life."

He ran a hand through thinning white hair, trying to find a way to make his friend understand.

"Falling Angel is my life. It used to be space. When I was a kid I read Heinlein and Doc Smith and Asimov and everything in between. I could foresee mankind spreading out through the solar system and into the stars, world after world until the stars themselves burn out—but I never thought I'd see it. Well, we're making it happen. I wish I could jump a thousand years and *see* . . . but in this age it's Falling Angel or nothing. This cable is our salvation. Someone needs to be here, right *here*, who understands everything about it. If that entails a certain degree of risk, then so be it. I placed myself under risk when I first became involved in the project. Things were a lot different in those days—we lost some good men and women. We all held a common dream, and we bet everything we had on it, and some lost."

"But you didn't have to come. You could

have sent Mannering, or—"

"No, no *no*. They are my assistants. Why are they my assistants? Because they are not qualified to run the department!"

"You've got to learn to delegate some responsibility—"

"Not with the cable. Not when it concerns the product I have spent *seven years* designing and extruding. Not when it spells the difference between life and death for Falling Angel. No!" Suddenly his voice was whiplash strong. "This is where I should be. I thought that you, of all people, would understand that. But if you don't, it's irrelevant. Whether you or anyone else understands doesn't matter at all."

"But Falling Angel needs you!"

"No. Not if I've done my work properly. If all goes well here, then Falling Angel has a new lease on life, and the younger people will have their chance to run things. Mannering is running things *now*, while I'm gone. The dinosaurs, me, Fleming—we won't matter. We got it going. The rest belongs to you. Would you have denied me this last chance to do my part?"

Thomas shook his head in confusion. "I just think . . ." His words dwindled away.

"Yes?"

"I just wish you didn't make it sound so final, that's all."

"That's my right, young man, and nobody else's. Now. What do you propose to do about all this?"

It was not instantly obvious that Thomas had lost his temper. "Oh, I suppose we'll have to turn around and take you back and start over after we load more cesium and more supplies. The conquest of the stars can wait a week and a half . . . no? *Dammit, Dexter!*"

Dexter was stunned speechless. It was as if his wallet had bitten his fingers.

"No, of course we can't turn around. It's just . . . you're my friend. Maybe my only friend, and I don't have the slightest idea how to keep you from committing suicide."

"It's not quite so bad as that," the giant said quietly. "I've merely made a decision that here, with my cable, is where I belong."

"All right. Well, Doctor, it looks like you're along for the ride. I hope you know what it is about you that scares me the most."

Dexter looked down into the round, almost petulant dark face, and nodded, laying a skeletally thin hand on Thomas's shoulder. "To see madness is one thing. But to see it and understand it too is a different breed of unicorn. We're all wild to conquer the stars, aren't we? I've just gone a little further over the line than you."

At last the smaller man smiled, a neutral twitch of the lips that grew warm in the light of Dexter's calm resolve.

"Good," Dexter said, slapping him on the shoulder. "Now . . . if we are finished here, shall we rejoin our companions above?"

Thomas prodded Dexter in the middle of the

chest with a stubby forefinger. "In eight hours. You're going to bed."

Stonecypher looked at him. "You sound just like Kelly."

"Someone has to. Do it."

Stonecypher nodded.

Seven

COURSE CHANGE

A day and a half out from Falling Angel, Stonecypher was looking better. At dinner he volunteered to take their meal trays down to the compactor. He started to turn . . . turned too far, lost his grip on one of the trays. Thomas noticed his sharp intake of breath, the wide-eyed puzzlement, the way his face lost color. Thomas frowned but did nothing. He didn't understand. Even after years in space, somehow one expects a heart attack victim to fall over.

Velcro slippers anchored Stonecypher's feet, but his body swayed like an undersea polyp while his mouth gaped and his fingers massaged his chest. Then the pressoreceptor reflex, a sympathetic reflex triggered by diminished arterial pressure, cut in, and increased the efficacy of the unaffected heart muscle, giving Stonecypher respite from the immediate agony.

Janet and Thomas reached him almost simultaneously, steadying, comforting. Marion was there a moment later. Feebly, he tried to push them away. "Damn it! I'm fine," he gasped. "Just need to catch my breath."

Marion was taking his pulse. "The hell you are. I think you're having a heart attack. Help me, Thomas?"

The metallurgist was hardly pretending to fight now; he needed all of his strength to breathe. They towed him headfirst down the ladder, and never bumped him once. He was still protesting while they hooked him up to the ship's diagnostic display.

· "Damn it, Dexter," Marion said nervously, waiting for Falling Angel to respond. "You, of all people, just aren't allowed to get sick on us."

The radio came to life. Three minutes: not bad. "This is Fleming at Falling Angel. Janet, how is he?"

"I'm not dead yet." Stonecypher opened his eyes. "Better. Better now." Janet was studying the diagnostic, and Stonecypher took a few minutes to breathe before attracting her attention. He reached out and found her hand, and tried to squeeze it. Perhaps only then did he fully appreciate how weak he was. "What's it say?"

The lightspeed gap was a second or so, but

Fleming's answer took longer than that. Fleming wasn't as calm as he tried to sound. "Bilateral cardiac failure, triggered by stress and deconditioning of the heart muscle. Dexter, the records show that you haven't kept up your aerobic points."

One of the metallurgist's frail hands gestured helplessly. "I've been busy."

"But *Dexter*—" Fleming caught himself, then spoke more softly. "All right, Dexter. We can talk about it later. The main question now is, what do we do with you? We *can't* let you go down to Earth."

Color came back into Dexter's face. "You don't have any choice, and it's stupid to even consider turning back—"

"Dexter, your *life*—"

The ailing man cursed, shaking with his frustration. "Fleming, if you do anything that impedes Falling Angel, don't you dare think you're doing it to help me. I'll be fine. You just get the cable pod into the Sea of Japan, and take *Anansi* down so we can deliver the other tools, and this old heart will heal just fine." His outburst seemed to drain him, and he sank back, coughing.

Thomas opened a small package into a silvery strip. He pulled it through the elastic lines that webbed his patient, then opened it further. It was a thin, heat-reflective blanket. Thomas spread it out beneath the web, tucked it around Stonecypher's chin, then his legs; his thin, knobby feet protruded out the far end, and Thomas cursed under his breath. He turned it into a wan smile. "Is there *anything* about you that's standard?"

Stonecypher tried to smile, gulping air. "You have to make allowances for genius."

Thomas tucked the edges in. Janet saw the tension shaping his round face into planes and angles. Stonecypher closed his eyes and breathed rhythmically, trying to relax.

Thomas took the microphone. "What are the chances of his condition being aggravated by descent into Earth's gravity well? Even if he lived through it . . ." Suddenly he didn't want to say the words. Stonecypher looked to be asleep, but he knew that within the still body was an active, worried mind. Whispering would make it worse. "How could he ever leave again? A liftoff would kill him for sure. He's spent the last eighteen years in low gravity."

Again, there was silence on the radio. Then Fleming said, "I don't see that we have a choice. Unless— Let me work on something."

Without opening his eyes, Stonecypher growled, "You don't have any choice at all. Let's stop this idle chatter and get on with our work. Or does anyone but me remember what that word means?"

"We know." Thomas was thinking hard. "But we do have an option. We can deliver the cable pod, then take Dexter home in *Anansi*."

Marion looked up, but Janet shook her head. "Thomas, *Anansi* doesn't have fuel to reach the Moon. We can maneuver in orbit—"

Marion jumped in with, "Can we use *Gabriel?* Without docking facilities?"

Thomas was nodding. "Shouldn't be a problem. That's what an ion drive tug *does:* it pushes a Shuttle between the Earth and the Moon. Docking facilities . . . hell, we'll just glue the push-pad to *Anansi*'s belly with the molecular glue in the cargo bay. God knows it's strong enough."

Fleming's radio voice said, "I thought maybe we could send you another Shuttle to take Dexter home, but it's no go. Haephestus is ready to go, but the tugs are tied up pushing *Lucifer* and *Susanoo*. *Lucifer* and *Susanoo* were launched from Ryukyu five days ago. They're almost back to Falling Angel; it'd take a week to send one of them back. There's nothing to bring him home except *Anansi*."

Stonecypher inhaled sharply. "The Japanese won't like that—"

"Screw the Japanese. They'll have the cable, they can wait two weeks for the rest. How fast can you get him home?"

Thomas closed his eyes. Relaxing tension turned clenched fists into hands; his moon-shaped face took on the full moon's sad calm. His mind was in the country of orbital mechanics now. Janet envied him this ability. Only by its absence did she realize the terrible strain he had been under.

Thomas said, "If we just turn around I could have him home in just over four days.

We're a day and a half out . . . another day and a half to decelerate, three more to get back to Falling Angel." Stonecypher tried to protest, and Janet laid a silencing finger against his lips. "If we make orbit and land the cable pod . . . call it seven days plus. It's faster coming home, without the mass of the cable pod." He licked his lips, and his breathing quickened as he juggled possibilities. "I can speed things up a little, too. Give me room—" He wedged himself past Dexter and the others to reach *Gabriel's* control board.

"I'll start up the fission plant and give us more power in the ion motors. We're carrying more cesium fuel than we need, too, because it's a test run—" He was talking rapidly now, holding conversation with himself.

Janet watched him with pride, excitement, and an irritating grain of jealousy.

Dexter stirred. "We should deliver the entire cargo. It's what Oyama paid for. Our reputation—"

The radio cut in again. "It looks like if he doesn't die in four days, he won't die in eight either. Dexter, I hate to say it, but you either stabilize or you don't. And we sure as hell can't have you dying during re-entry. Did you give one second's thought to the *publicity* when you pulled this stunt?"

"That's not my department," Dexter laughed raggedly.

"Thomas, how are you doing?"

"Ask me again in a couple of hours,

Fleming. This *is* a trial run. But I've got the fission plant running in tandem with the solar power cells, which gives me more electrical power in the grids that ionize the cesium, which lets me increase the cesium flow too. That gets us better than half again as much thrust. If everything works I can get us to Earth-orbit eight hours early. Back to Falling Angel in seven days one hour not counting the time it takes to land the cable pod and moor *Anansi* and *Gabriel*."

"I know you'll do your best. Dexter, if you wanted to be a martyr, couldn't you do it at home?"

A faint chuckle bubbled out of Stonecypher's throat. "Nope. Damned Kelly always gets in the way. Had to get away from her—" He began to cough, the racking sounds shaking his thin frame and cutting off his words.

"All right. Marion, keep his heart and vital functions monitored. Dexter, you do nothing but rest for seven days. By then we'll have you in the best hospital in the solar system, the only one with pacemakers and free fall too."

Djalma Costa awakened quickly, as he had learned to do in the past week. Coming overland from Mehrabad he had first felt it, the little sourness in the stomach, the touch of cool air at the back of the neck, the pre-conscious thrill that warned of danger.

His hosts treated him well, but Hoveida especially had eyes which questioned. Too often the conversation had drifted innocently to BTE's other business concerns, to questions concerning the programming of the missile.

Costa could honestly deny access to technical information. He wondered if they believed him.

And tension had grown. The men of the United Muslim Activist Front provided manpower: moving the machinery, constructing the launch site and the camouflaged bivoac. Then there were the men sent by BTE, the actual technicians who would direct the assembly of missile and scaffolding, who would send it streaking into the heavens on a grim rendezvous. There were twice as many Muslims as BTE personnel, and the primarily Brazilian technicians kept to themselves.

Except for Djalma. From the first, Hoveida had made sure that the little man was near to hand, that he slept nearer the Muslims than the Brazilians. That a "bodyguard" be with him at all times.

That the constant, small prickle of fear continue to grow.

So Costa awakened in his tent, his eyes opened to a slit, and he assessed the room. There was someone in the tent. A shallow stream of light shone under the tent flap, and Costa could make out an outline. "Hoveida?"

The terrorist's voice was very low and calm. "All is prepared. We need to talk."

Costa nodded in the dark. "I'll be with you

in a moment."

The head, a dull oval in the dim light, inclined in agreement. The tall man left the tent.

Costa pulled himself upright and realized that he was shaking. "Damn!" he whispered, rubbing thin shoulders. Why did Hoveida have to have the same impact on him every time? His body was misted with cold sweat, and once again it seemed that the room temperature had dropped.

"Get hold of yourself," he told himself softly, pulling on pants and shoes. "Today's the day." That thought seemed to banish the fears. Soon he would be through with this phase of the project, and on to a more familiar, and rewarding, phase.

He emerged from his tent a moment later. The sun was still an orange ball on the horizon, and had not yet cut the chill from the air. He looked out across the flat, packed sand of the Iranian Central Plateau, past the clusters of brown and dull green tents and huts, to the towering shape of the Prometheus missile, held in the skeletal embrace of its scaffolding.

Bathed in the warm light of the morning sun it seemed a thing of beauty, not destruction, and for a moment all seemed right with the world. Then he remembered his place and purpose. He hurried to the main hut.

Hoveida and Mansur were there, dressed in brown fatigues. Mansur was scribbling notes on the last sheet of a stack in front of him. He

folded the rest of the sheets back down and
squared the pile and shoved it toward the
center of the green metal table. "This project
is somewhat different from those I have been
involved with in the past." Again, it was difficult to decipher his words, so thick was his
accent. "But the basic idea is the same. We
wish to relay an explosive charge to a vulnerable area. It matters little if the courier is a
truck, the postal service, a child on a bicycle,
or—" He gestured in the direction of the
Prometheus. "—a guided missile."

He drummed his fingers on the table, then
looked at Costa. "There are many things that I
do not understand about the guidance system
of your rocket. There has been little time for
exchange of ideas between my team and
yours. At times I have wondered if this was
deliberate." His eyes flared, and Djalma felt
the impact of his suspicion. Then the eyes
were hooded again, and Mansur went on.
"However, if your people have performed in
all respects as I know mine have, then we are
totally prepared. We are monitoring the con-
versations between Falling Angel and Oyama
Construction, so we will know when *Anansi*
has moved into orbit.

"If I understand the procedure correctly,
Anansi will send the cable on ahead,
monitoring its entry path. They are planning
for splashdown in the Sea of Japan. It will be
simple for us to monitor their position." For
the first time the ghost of a smile played on

Mansur's face, a touch of pride in craft. "When this day is done, it will have opened a new era. This is . . . history."

Hoveida grunted, but his lips were curled in a smile. "Your people will be ready by sunset. We expect *Anansi* to establish orbit at that time. And then . . ." Now the smile was savage, predatory, so that Mansur laughed aloud. "Then the bird will fly."

Costa waited the laughter out. "And by that time, the men will be ready to disperse?"

"Of course. And the announcement of the attack will be made from Mehrabad." Hoveida's long fingers played through his beard. There was real pleasure in that angular face now. "The world will learn of our power." Then, with a touch of mischief, "But not of our friends."

"Good, good." Djalma looked at his watch. "There is much to be done. If you will excuse me . . .?" He turned to the door. He had reached it, and was halfway through when he heard Hoveida's voice, softer than usual.

"Mr. Costa! Your money has paid for this—" He waved his hand vaguely. "All of this, and it has not been cheap. I hope that you enjoy the show."

The small man nodded, smiled briefly, and left the hut. The sun was higher in the sky, brighter, hotter. It would be hotter still before the day was done. But everything was moving on schedule . . .

Jorge Xavier had not slept for two nights. Again he lay alone in his bed, sleeping blinders snugly fitted to his eyes, two tranquilizer pills dissolving in his stomach.

And his wide-awake mind played with details, extrapolating and inverting logical constructs and examining minutiae with fanatic thoroughness.

Something was wrong. Some factor had changed, and was as yet unaccounted for. Information. With precise, accurate information, adjustments could be made, disaster averted, errors rectified. But something had been lost. He could feel it. It kept him awake and staring into the blackness of his night, turning the known over and over in a fruitless search for the unknown.

He ran a hand through his hair, feeling the cold, sticky perspiration that clogged his scalp.

In a few hours, when the final phase of the project came into play, Brazil Techimetal-Electromotores president Castellon would certainly learn of Xavier's plotting, and the final power-play would begin. If he was as intelligent as Xavier thought, Castellon would wait to learn the outcome of Xavier's gamble. If it was successful, he would not bring the law into the matter; that would destroy BTE's salvage claim to the cable. He would surely wait and attempt to ease Xavier out of the company before the younger man could challenge his leadership. Xavier was prepared to fight that, prepared to prove to the stock-holders that it was his own decisive action that had saved the company from Castellon's craven timidity.

Xavier smiled at that thought. He welcomed an open battle for power.

But if the plan failed . . .

Failed *how?* A fresh wave of nausea and fatigue flushed his system, sweat beading his forehead. *How? I know people. I know where they will go if prodded here, tempted there, threatened, rewarded . . . my own people, Castellon, the Arab fanatics, the Japanese . . . though they will do nothing at all, for what can they do? Like the men of space—*

There it was: the men of space were not like the men he knew. It wasn't his country, this factory complex falling around and around the Moon, with death waiting outside every wall . . . Xavier knew how to move people, but these people he did not know.

What they *could* do was nothing, he had seen to that—

The telephone buzzed, and Xavier rolled over to push the intercom button, all in one galvanic spasm. "Yes?"

"Da Silva." The financier's voice was low, urgent, and Xavier propped himself nearer the speaker, tearing away his blinders. Faint light streamed in through his apartment window, the distant blinking of a neon bill-board. "We have received a message from Yamada."

All fatigue fell away from Xavier. "Continue."

"He is aboard the Oyama flagship in the Sea of Japan, as you know. Two days ago, they received word that Dr. Dexter Stonecypher, the metallurgist who developed the cable, has fallen ill."

Xavier felt a momentary fury at being wakened for such trivia. Then the thought clicked into place: "He's aboard the Shuttle, isn't he?"

"Yes. *Anansi* has made plans to get back to Falling Angel as soon as possible. They will be making orbit, and dropping the package, approximately eight hours early."

"Eight . . ." He sat bolt upright. "Have you alerted Costa yet? The Prometheus—it must be launched early. *Have you?*"

"Of course, Xavier," Da Silva protested. "But the time lag—"

"Why?" he screamed. "How did this happen?"

"Oyama is being very cautious, and maintaining radio silence. It took two days for Yamada to put a cipher message through to his mistress, who relayed it to us."

Two days . . . eight hours . . . "I'm coming in," Xavier said, rolling off the bed and finding his slippers in the dark. "Patch any new information through to me as soon as it arrives."

"Yes sir."

Xavier paused for a moment at his window,

opened his blinds to look out over the night-dark, jeweled city.

So. Trouble. He did not doubt or question the instinct that had warned him, as it had warned him so many times before. Such, he felt sure, were the faculties of superior men, of warriors. Winners.

He pulled the blinds closed and drew on a robe. There was nothing to do but act, now, driving all uncertainties from his mind with an iron will. That, too, was the mark of a superior man.

Thomas stood on a broad icy plain, its horizon shrouded in mist. There were no mountains, no distinct clouds, no sound. He looked for landmarks: there were none. He walked and never moved, the horizon receding perfectly, evenly, until it seemed he was merely strolling in place, the ice stealing his traction.

He knew that there was a reason for him to be there. It would reveal itself if he could only think about it long enough. Slowly, with infinite patience, the patience of the hunter in his blood, he sat upon the ice and waited.

There was a sound. He looked up, into the white-hazed sky, and saw a streak of greater light arcing down from the heavens, cleaving the mists, boiling away the vapor and leaving clear blue sky behind. It was coming directly at him now, but he merely saw and watched even as his instinct screamed for him to run.

Why run? I cannot move.

It was closer now, and the closer it came the slower it seemed to move: a fireball that wailed its unliving pain as it fell. It struck the ice directly in front of him and before it struck he could almost see what it was. It wasn't lifeless at all. It seemed to be a face, or faces, and the more he strained to see the features behind the flame, the more it blurred. The ice shattered in slow-motion, steam and flame and screams of agony melding together—

Janet was touching his shoulder, her face, beautiful and pale, very close to his. Her fingers touched his forehead and came away wet. "You were dreaming," she said.

He blinked, looked around the room carefully: the lockers, the kitchenette, Dexter hanging suspended in his blanket like a bat sleeping with furled wings. He unbuckled his web with a shaking hand, pushed himself away from it. In three seconds the uncertainty and fear were gone from his face, wiped away like numbers from a slate. "Nightmare," he said, his voice already calm.

He floated over to Dexter. The metallurgist wore a pressure suit helmet now, in lieu of an oxygen mask. His breathing sounded ragged and hollow. In the three days since the heart attack they had watched the monitors edge from "serious" to "moderate" and back again. He watched the movement of the chart lines, his stomach heavy and hot.

Again, Janet's hand grasped his shoulder. "Tommy, are you all right?"

"I was alone." He said quietly, almost as if he were speaking to the machine, "I knew there was something wrong, but there was nothing I could do. All I could do was wait." He turned and looked at her, looked past her to Dexter, cocooned in silver. "Something bad was coming, Janet, and when it came, it screamed and burned." He glanced back at the readouts, then at the digital clock over the microwave range. "And all I could do was watch. And wait." He tried to smile. "I'm all right. Just a little tense, I guess. Three hours to orbit." He turned up the wattage on his smile and it came alive at last. "Even if *Gabriel* glitched on us now, we could still get the cable pod down. The program would be hairier, that's all. Who's going to EVA with me, you or Marion?"

"Marion. I'll stay with the Shuttle. Deploying the cable pod is no big deal, you know, and we don't have to do anything else till it's down in the Sea of Japan."

She took his hands, and the gentleness there almost frightened him, some proud child in his mind saying *I'm not a basket case. Keep your sympathy—*

But he didn't pull away. "This hasn't been good, Tommy," she said. "I had hoped that this time together might be—" she shook her head, trying to find the words. "Well, if not healing, at least soothing. Pleasant. You

know, the two of us doing something important together."

"We are."

"You know what I'm saying. This trip is
really the end for us and . . . and I hoped that
. . ." Her voice tailed off. "I don't know. I
guess I wish it hadn't been quite like this."

He watched her, his dark mongol face
changing not at all as he tried to choose
among the thoughts that swirled competi-
tively in his head. "It was good for us for
awhile, Janet. That's more than a lot of people
have." He squeezed her hands fondly. "Hell—
it's more than *I* ever expected. Anyway, you
didn't really expect a second honeymoon
here? Where would we get the privacy?"

She laughed: not humor, just nerves.

He leaned forward and kissed her mouth,
gently refusing the invitation of her parted
lips. He pulled his hand free and stood. "I've
got work to do," he said without a trace of
cruelty.

She nodded and started up the ladder to the
command level, turning to watch him working at his console. She knew that she had already vanished from his world, replaced by
the unliving and intangible. She didn't,
couldn't, begrudge him that ability. If anything, it was the basis of much of her respect
for him, if not her love.

The sight of Stonecypher touched off a
sudden pang. Thomas was grieving more for
the loss of that old man than for the loss of

their marriage. She allowed herself the luxury of hating herself for that impulse. It was a small thought, an unworthy one. But it was real.

Perhaps he was right: it was too late to say anything. They would act out the rest of their roles, and take their bows.

Still she felt old, tired, and the strain of the past three days hammered at the gates of her control. She shouted it down. *Not now. Not for another week.* But when this was all over, she knew that she was going to find someone to curl up with and find peace—

No. She would find a place to be by herself, and she would find her own peace. She glided up the ladder, feeling . . . not heavy, but massive, her mind and spirit swollen almost beyond tolerance.

The Earth was flowing beneath them now: fingerpaint clouds swirled in fluffy spirals on a blue-on-blue worldscape, sunglare blazing off the deep blue patch of the Mediterranean. Thomas talked to himself out loud, keeping them posted:

"I've got the nuclear pile damped. Thrust dropping . . . Turning the solar panels . . . got them edgewise now, going to batteries. Velocity seven point one two two KPS. Seven one zero zero and I'm cutting the cesium flow. Thrust is zero. We're in orbit. You're in charge."

"Good," Janet called from the flight deck.

"Marion, make the call."

There was satisfaction in Marion's voice. "Oyama, this is *Anansi*. *Anansi* to *Oyama*. We are in orbit at seven point one zero zero kilometers per second, altitude one four seven oh kilometers. We'll be deploying the cable pod immediately."

The voice that came back was dry and cultured, and relayed from the Sea of Japan by satellite. "Oyama Flagship One. We are tracking. Our present position is approximately two hundred miles southwest of Akita. Anticipate splashdown in two hours ten minutes, at eleven hundred sixteen hours, Tokyo time. Falling Angel has kept us well abreast of your progress. Most eager to receive package."

"You're aware that *Anansi* will *not* be going down?"

"We were informed. Please convey our sympathies to Dr. Stonecypher."

"Will do. We'll keep the line open."

A smile, the first warm one in days, was spreading across Janet's face. "Home stretch."

Marion Guiness watched an ugly smear of white, a frosty fingerprint of cloud, inching toward them on the great blue disk. He grunted, eyes narrowed a fraction. "Anticyclonic clouds—off Portugal there."

Janet studied it for a second. "Looks nasty. Don't think it will affect our drop much . . . but we better make sure that's programmed into the weather model."

"That's ground control's job. I'll mention it though."

Thomas's head poked up through the ladder well. "How long do I have?"

"To suit up? Just as soon as I do this." One button on Marion's keyboard was surrounded by a tiny metal cage. He flipped it back and pressed. *Anansi* shuddered.

"What was *that?*"

Thomas laughed. "I just cut us loose from the cable pod. It's the same key that blows away the main tank supports during a launch. That's why it's in that little cage. You don't want to jog it with your elbow."

He was tapping at the keyboard as he spoke, and *Anansi* continued to shudder. The cargo bay doors opened, quite evenly. Marion held attitude jet keys down, and the view through the windows swung smoothly: Earth, then stars, then the cable pod and ion drive, still linked, off to their right.

"I'll just bring us up close enough that we can use tethers," Marion said. "We can go out through the cargo bay." The cable pod and ion drive drifted past, then halted at another touch of the keys. "*Now* let's get dressed. Janet, take over?"

"I relieve you. Luck."

Thomas guided himself over to the lockers. He pulled his pressure suit out on its rack and plugged it in for a computer diagnostic. While that was going on he gave it a careful visual inspection. Satisfied, De Camp unzipped the front and backed in. There were zippers everywhere, and it took a limber man to get them all closed. Then it hugged him like a sausage skin. He pulled the fishbowl helmet over his head and clamped it down.

Marion was still suiting up. De Camp waited until his partner's helmet was on, then switched on his microphone. "How you doing?"

"Raise your volume a little."

"Now?"

"Fine." Marion turned to the airlock, using the magnets on his boots. He cycled through the airlock into the cargo bay. Thomas spared a glance at the sleeping Stonecypher. Have to keep him calm somehow, once he realised that they'd let him sleep through this. *It's going to be fine*, he said silently. *You'll see*.

He waited until the warning light turned green, then followed.

The sound of the pump died to silence. He stepped into the cargo bay. It was packed with sealed and bundled packages of all sizes, headed for Oyama Construction—eventually. They would have to wait until the next trip.

Marion was strapping himself into one of the chair-shaped mobility packs, and Thomas was right behind him. He checked the pack's circuits, then spared a glance up out of the bay. The Earth hung there, a dark swollen disk filling the sky.

"Ready?"

"Go."

In tandem, silently, the two men arced up and around until they cleared the wings.

The ion drive/cable pod combination hung close alongside. Everything looked fine. Thomas ran through his mental checklist. *Anything wrong? Ten limpet motors mounted in place, undisturbed. No obvious meteor pocks*...and what else *could* go wrong? The cable pod had been inert cargo till now.

Okay. Detach the mating rings. Separate the cable pod from the ion drive. Then back to the ship, check the cameras and other instruments, and send it on down.

The night-shrouded Earth formed a velvet-black backdrop. Here and there cities glowed; tiny sparks of lightning showed in the storm off Portugal.

"Ready?"

"Give me a moment," Marion said happily. "I never could resist a sunrise."

The sun flared into view: a sudden white crescent glowed along the Earth's eastern rim. A tiny brightness showed above Iran, floated into the daylit area and was gone.

"Moving out," Thomas said. He jumped at the black Earth. His safety tether trailed back from him in loops.

"Thomas, did you see anything out there? I thought I caught a flare of some kind."

Let's get the job done, daydreamer. "Where?"

"High in the atmosphere . . . Janet, did you

see it?"

"No."

Thomas whistled low, in irritation. "All right, I'll take a look." He had almost reached the mating rings, where the ion drive joined the cable pod. Now his backpack jets flared and he veered away, behind *Gabriel*. "Okay, where?"

Marion sounded almost petulant. "It *was* there. I saw it."

Thomas closed his eyes and counted to five. "Right. Now can we get on with the—" The mating rings exploded, searing his vision white as the world turned to fire and pain.

Eight

DAMAGE REPORT

His head snapped away reflexively, not quickly enough to miss it. Before Thomas' polarizer cut in a terrifying image was burned into his retinae: light arcing, coiling around the cable pod like sentient lightning.

Something that felt like a wall of water smashed into his chest. The cable pod dropped below his line of sight, still spitting fire. Then *Anansi*, off to the side, seemed to explode in flame.

Hissing static filled his helmet, painfully loud. After the first moment of shock he regained control of his voice. "Marion! Do you copy? Repeating—"

Space had turned foggy around him. *Anansi*'s outline, blurred and dimmed to dark blue by the visor, whirled past his field of vision. There were flame-colors in the fog around *Anansi*, red and blue and yellow, dimming as they ballooned outward. *Pretty*, he thought. Flame in vacuum. He'd seen rocket exhausts, but never anything like this.

I'm tumbling! His fingers tapped at controls on his chest, and hot gasses jetted from his mobility unit. He didn't need his brain for this. He could have stopped a tumble in his sleep. "Marion, do you copy?"

There was a spitting sound, and a stress-tautened voice rang through the static. "Tommy! This is *Anansi*." Janet's voice gained control even as he listened. *Good girl.* "Bad trouble here. Something gave us a hell of a wallop—" There was a string of words obscured by hissing, and *Anansi* passed his field of vision again. "I've lost some external sensors—don't think cabin integrity has been compromised—"

He'd killed the tumble.

Janet paused, then spoke again. "Tommy—relaying message from Marion."

There was a click, and Thomas could hear Guiness' breathing, heavy in his ear. "Thomas?"

"Here, Marion. About a hundred meters off *Anansi*. It looks pretty bad." The fog was thinning, dispersing in vacuum, the fire-colors gone. The explosion had separated the cable pod from *Gabriel*. Re-entry shielding had peeled up around the tail of the cable pod, and a cloud of white mist surrounded the ion drive, and the solar panels— "The ion drive's the worst. The solar panels are shredded, and I think the cesium tank must have been ripped open. The cable pod—"

"Are *you* all right?"

De Camp gritted his teeth. "I'm all right— just shaken up and—" His ears popped. Horrified, he listened for a hissing sound— and heard it. "Damn." His voice went icy calm, freezing in an instant. "I think I have a leak here . . ." His visor had cleared and he checked himself over. The rip was two inches above his knee. It was small, and the edges were bubbling as the silicone self-seal frothed into action. "Minor—class one, maybe. Suit is sealing, but I'm going to put a patch on it. Where are you?" Thomas took one of the flat, flexible repair patches from his side pouch. The accustomed clumsiness of his gloves frightened him now, with the wound in his suit bubbling air. He bit into his lip and forced his fingers to obey, peeling off the protective backing and smoothing the patch into place.

"I have visual contact with you, Thomas. We're about equidistant from the cable pod, but I'm further astern. My suit-to-suit is out, that's why it took me a second to reroute through Janet. I think my mobility unit took a hit. Sharpnel, I guess . . . I'm tumbling. What the hell *happened?*"

The hissing sound had stopped. Thomas scanned *Anansi*. She was spinning around a

skew axis. No obvious damage to the belly . . .
none to the nose . . . she turned, and Thomas'
heart sank at what had happened to the
Shuttle's tail. The aft Reaction Control System
pod on the left was ripped open and half
melted. The fuel and oxydizer tanks must
have ripped and exploded. That was the fireball.
The RCS pod on the right looked undamaged.
The vertical fin . . . blackened by
fire.

Janet said, "I'm trying to stop *Anansi*'s spin,
but I don't get anything from either of the aft
RCS systems. Trying the forward module . . .
ah." It looked like steam venting from
Anansi's nose. "I'm killing our spin."

The cable pod was worse hit. The fins were
twisted, ruined; the heat-shielding had peeled
upward in shards. What about the precious
cable itself? He couldn't tell.

Fragments were still spinning in all directions,
and everything still looked foggy with
gasses and bits of metal. He finally picked out
Marion's tiny form, looking much like a man
strapped into a metal chair. *A crippled man*,
Thomas thought. He aimed himself toward
Marion and used the mobility unit thrusters.

His course took him past the cable pod and
Gabriel, slowly drifting apart. He was able to
spot more damage. The mating rings were
still mated, still part of the cable pod, but
splayed and melted, as if they had been
packed with Thermite. Most of the limpet
motors had been blown into the sky; a couple

still clung, in skewed positions. Some of the silica heat-shield bricks on the rear underside of the Shuttle had been torn free.

He was running out of safety tether. Marion's must have been severed. The copilot was even now floating further and further from *Anansi*. Thomas hurriedly unhooked his own line before it could snap taut, and continued after him.

What in hell happened? He remembered Marion's words, " . . . a flare of some kind . . . high in the atmosphere . . ." and cursed himself for his disbelief. Guiness was a competent, trained observer, and Thomas made a mental note never to let personal feelings twist his judgement again.

Marion was still tumbling. Thomas watched his distance closing, and used mobility unit jets to slow himself a bit. "Hang in there, Marion."

"Haven't got a lot of choice. I can't get a good look at *Anansi*. How is she?"

Janet's voice cut in. "I've lost my rear attitude jets. Have to use the front primary and vernier thrusters, but it's slow and—oh, my God."

Her voice had gone from cold to frightened, and the sudden loss of clarity sent a knife point of anxiety into Thomas' gut. He could feel beads of sweat blossoming on his face. Ahead, within the metal-vapor mist, was Marion, turning helplessly.

"I just got a warning from Dexter's life

support. His blood pressure's dropping. I think he's going into cardiogenic shock."

The sweat droplets itched, and Thomas shook his head reflexively. The globules scattered, spattering into his faceplate and breaking into spray. A droplet hit his eye, burning. The suit responded to increased heat: a cool breeze blew up from his chin.

"His heart's giving out?"

"Yes, dammit, and I can't leave the controls. Get Marion in as soon as you can, he can see to Dexter while you check out the exterior damage."

Thomas gritted his teeth and adjusted his course slightly, preparing to move alongside Marion. The copilot was doll-sized now, a silver-white figure spinning slowly against a vast darkness edged with a thick crescent of white cloud and blue water. "Did you hear that, Marion?"

"God, yes. I'd like to think there's something I can do, but I don't know. Everything's happening at once."

"Just hold on." Thomas snatched at Marion's hand as he spun past. He caught the back of Marion's wrist, then lost his grip. That left Thomas himself rotating. He used jets to kill the rotation and got back to Marion, who had shed some spin. Again Thomas caught his passing arm, held on against the recoil, felt Marion's hand close on his wrist. They jerked and spun. Thomas used the gas jets until they were both facing back toward *Anansi*.

"Man," Marion said as he righted himself. "Am I glad to see you."

"I hope you have your triple-A paid up. We're a long way from the nearest tow station."

"Take a check?"

Thomas hugged Marion from the back, to balance them, and headed back toward the crippled Shuttle. His eyes picked up the ruined aft section of the cable pod, and he snarled. They *needed* Dexter Stonecypher.

Marion heard the hiss of returning atmosphere in the lock, and his mind raced in a dozen directions at once. Damage . . . how much damage? And where? The cable pod was a ruin. It couldn't leave orbit . . . and most of the limpet motors were gone too.

The ion drive? Have to see, but with the cesium fuel tank ripped apart, *Gabriel* was surely unuseable. *Anansi?* Both aft RCS pods damaged, and what else? The vertical fin? Could *Anansi* move at all?

We could be marooned.

The ready light blinked green, and he swung the inner door open. Thoughts of material problems disappeared as he saw Dexter, anchored by blanket and electronic sensors. The metallurgist was in pain, shuddering, gasping for breath, and although he faced the opening door his eyes didn't focus.

Marion doffed his helmet and pulled himself over to his patient. He checked the life support readout and swore. With desperate speed he flipped the intercom to "on" and barked up to Janet. "Marion here. How long have Dexter's signs been running crazy?"

"Check the computer. I'm still evening out the spin." She didn't say, *I'm busy, damn you!*, but he heard it in her voice.

He danced his fingers over the controls. The diagnostic readout board cleared, then began to display. Marion said something foul.

Dexter groaned, eyes focusing at last on Marion. 'Who's there . . .?" he asked weakly.

The copilot watched the red and green graphics as the computer fed Stonecypher cardiotonic drugs, mechanically seeking to stave off irreversible shock. Dexter's voice, pitiable in its weakness, tore at him.

"Who's there?" The elder scientist's thin hand stretched out, grasping at air, and brushed Marion's shoulder. "Cynthia?" Marion heard pain, and loneliness, and need. He kept his face turned away, watching the flickering lights and sliding graphics that measured out the remaining moments of Stonecypher's life. The hand on his shoulder tugged again, weakly, and the copilot grasped it gently and turned back.

Stonecypher's eyes were glazed, his face wracked with strain. He labored for every breath, sweat standing out from his forehead in jeweled beads. His body shook, and the droplets spun off into the air, drifting as slowly as tiny soap bubbles.

"Cynthia? Oh God, it hurts!"

"It's Marion, Doc." He wiped Stonecypher's forehead. "You're on board *Anansi*."

The older man's eyes focused, and just for an instant he was there, really there in the Shuttle, a man who was weak, and pale, but lucid. "*Anansi*. What happened?" He grew more intense. "There was an explosion. Is the cable all right? Is . . .?" He gasped for air, groaning as if his chest were bound tight with chains.

"Yes," Marion lied, remembering the blackened, ruptured cable pod. After all, the cable itself *might* be undamaged, though they wouldn't be sure until Thomas finished his report. "Everything's fine. You just relax."

"Yes . . ." His eyes drifted shut, even as his body shivered in pain. "I thought . . . I thought that Cynthia was here, but of course she wouldn't be." His voice was becoming slurred. "Tell her. Tell her and the grandchildren." One eyelid opened again, and the eye looked filmy, its light dimmed. "Never saw them. Only pictures. Never went back. Cynthy . . . only daughter . . . you'd think . . ." and the eye shut again.

Stonecypher's hand had gone limp, horribly so. Marion checked the blood pressure reading. "Sixty over forty," he murmured, and felt the snarl distort his face. He felt so helpless!

The diagnostic display read, "80.00 poss ventricular tacycardia," and as the metallurgist's body relaxed with dreadful finality, Marion felt his sight blur. He fumbled for a tissue. Crying was a mistake in free fall; the tear built up into a single salty globule over the eye.

Stonecypher's body, anchored by its sensors and tubes and safety strap, remained upright after the display buzzed dully and flashed red, after there was no more movement. And no more pain.

"Falling Angel, this is *Anansi*." Janet was steady now, as steady as the ship itself. The attitude jets in the nose had finally slowed the spin, and Earth's disk no longer whirled crazily past their windows.

"We read you, *Anansi*. Request preliminary status report."

In cold, precise words Janet recited the litany of torn metal and flesh that screamed to her from the dials and cathode ray displays. She repeated what Thomas had seen on his preliminary inspection.

When she was finished she ran her fingers through her hair and calmed herself, feeling shakier than she cared to admit. There was the sound of cloth rustling against metal, and she heard Marion sigh. From the corner of her eye she saw the medical readout flashing red, and her head dropped.

Marion laid a slender hand on her shoulder. She saw his reflection, faint in the front window, as he shook his head in grim negation.

He moved stiffly to his seat and immersed himself in the silent testimony of the read-outs.

"Crew status," Janet said, her voice rough and too low. She cleared her throat, and the words became crisp and professional. "Crew status. Pilot De Camp and Copilot Guiness are unharmed. Ion Tech De Camp took a class one suit breech, was able to affect repair. He escorted Guiness to the lock, and is returning to the cable pod for full inspection."

"Was he injured?"

"Not enough to stop him from going back out." She paused, switching mental tracks from her concern for her husband. "Metallurgist Stonecypher experienced terminal heart failure, apparently due to stress caused by the explosion."

The next voice on the line was Fleming himself, and he spoke with emotionless precision. "Can you describe the nature of the explosion?"

Marion leaned forward to the microphone. "I saw it, but I'm not sure I can describe it for you. There was a flash high in the atmosphere a few seconds before we were hit. Tentative hypothesis: missile attack of some sort. Never seen anything like that impact, though."

"Can you clarify?"

"The missile never came near us." He squinted, even the memory taxing his ability to communicate. Nothing like this had ever happened. "It was a bright flash, but tens of

kilometers below us. Maybe there was
another missile, but . . ."

"Well?"

"No, dammit, it wasn't enough. A missile
the size of the one we saw would have blown
us all to gas. What *hurt* us was an explosion
between the ion drive and the cable pod. It
looked a little like napalm, or ball lightning.
No . . ." He squeezed his eyes shut trying to
remember clearly. "The explosion seemed to
crawl along the joining, spreading like the
threads of a spiderweb. And it ripped up
everything in its path. This was deliberate,
and precise, and damned sophisticated. No
missile could have done it. A mine. Maybe in
the mating rings themselves."

Janet watched the tension turn his face
ugly, and knew that she wasn't the only one
battling to retain equilibrium. There was
nothing more for her to do up top, but she had
a crawling hunger to do something, anything,
useful. "Relieve me?" she asked.

Marion nodded. "What now?"

"We have work to do, and we won't be able
to do it with Dr. Stonecypher's body down
there. I'm going to . . . I don't know. Put him
in his suit, I guess. Then take him into the
bay." She knew what he was about to ask, and
touched his hand. "No, I can take care of
this myself. I need you up here. Be careful,
Marion, and let me know if anything changes."

Nine

THE GOOD NEIGHBOR POLICY

Fleming sat, deadly silent, as the computer-animated *Anansi* went through her holographic paces. The damage to Shuttle and cargo pod was outlined in red: the ion drive was swathed in it.

Connors was there in the darkened room. Like De Camp, he was an ion drive technician and operator, though he claimed other skills too. He was a smallish beach ball of a man who kept to the low and null-grav sections of Falling Angel as much as possible. He was watching the cable pod burn.

Aerodynamics altered drastically, the grey oval began to glow soon after it reached the upper atmosphere. He watched as the foamed ceramic peeled off in blazing droplets, then chunks. The ruined fins had no hope of stabilizing its descent, and when the drogue chute finally popped free it was in tatters within seconds, a pitiful white streamer spattered with flaming ceramic and metal.

It impacted somewhere in the Pacific.

The lights came up in the room, and Fleming spoke quietly. "Thank you, Kelly. Join us, please."

"On my way." There was a brittle note in Kelly's voice, as if she were biting down hard on the words.

He swivelled in his chair, fingers steepled, peering over them at Connors. "Accurate?"

"Only too. There's no way in the world we're going to get that pod down without repair. And that's a chancy job. The patching material is going to change either mass or configuration." He thought for a moment. "We'll have to check the possibility of pushing Stonecypher's foam projector out to them. Any ideas?"

"One big one. *Susanoo* will be in in an hour, and that gives us an ion drive tug, *Michael*. You'll have to take *Michael* down to bring *Anansi* home. Any reason you can't push the foam factory down at the same time? I'll tell Strickland. I want a crew putting that package together quick."

The door shushed and Kelly was there, clothes thrown on roughly and hair unkempt. She seemed to be moving by nervous energy alone.

Stonecypher's death was hitting her hard.

Fleming had considered taking her off duty, giving her time to grieve. But Kelly was *in* this; it was her fight too, and her right to see it won or lost. And . . . she was needed.

He said, "Get me a line to Oyama, Kelly."

"There's something coming in on their frequency now, Doctor." She strode past him to her console, switched the transmission into the room. The holo cameras in the ceiling focused on Fleming.

Patches of light formed and congealed. The Japanese was a stranger, dressed in a dark, European-style business suit. He jerked out of his thoughtful, dreaming pose when Falling Angel's image reached him. "Mr. Fleming? I am Izumi, and I speak for Oyama Construction."

"Yes, Mr. Izumi. We are receiving you clearly."

"Good." But Izumi looked grim. "Approximately eight minutes ago, the following transmission was broadcast world wide, from one of the commercial satellites. The point of origin seems to have been Iran. Hold, please."

The air fuzzed for a few seconds; then a woman's face appeared. She was definitely middle-eastern, and her hair was pulled back severely. The transmission seemed shaky.

"Taped under bad conditions," Conners muttered.

"Nations of the world!" Her English was thick and studied. "We, the United Muslim

Activist Front, have struck a great blow for
freedom. Today we have proven that there is
nowhere on Earth—" here she paused for
dramatic effect. "Nor in the sky where the
cowardly lackies of capitalism can hide from
the wrath of the people.

"Today, using a surface-to-orbit missile of
highly advanced capabilities, we attacked and
destroyed the Space Shuttle *Anansi*. We
grieve for the loss of lives. This tragedy was
made necessary by the limitless greed of the
capitalist nations, to warn them that they will
not despoil the Earth and leave us a bitter
husk. We will fight for our lands, and we will
fight for our skies." She raised a khaki-clad
arm, making a tight fist. "Long live the revolu-
tion!"

She faded from the screen.

"A Prometheus?" Connors asked incredu-
lously.

"More likely the Soviet version." Fleming
fell silent, watching the projection point.

The air fogged again, and Retsudo Oyama
appeared. He seemed grimly alert, though
there was a pink puffiness to his eyes . . .
What was it, five in the morning down there?
He said, "I hardly need to tell you of my
concern, Mr. Fleming. I need to know: How
accurate are the claims of the UMAF?"

"There has been damage to *Anansi*, but she
hasn't been destroyed. We . . . lost one of the
crew. Dr. Stonecypher, the mind responsible
for the cable."

Retsudo's forehead furrowed. "I am very sorry. He was a great man. I hope—" he paused, trying to phrase his words delicately. "I hope his final work was not destroyed."

"Preliminary reports indicate that the cable pod was damaged. One of the crew, Thomas De Camp, is investigating more closely now. We hope to have a favorable report within the hour."

The younger Oyama's head bobbed fractionally. "As to the nature of the attack . . ."

"Yes?"

"As an industrial nation dependent upon foreign resources for our raw materials, Japan has suffered its share of terrorism. We have had brushes with the UMAF before. Never have they displayed the technical skill necessary to accomplish this feat."

Fleming glanced at Kelly and Conners. "Yes . . . but we can't say that they actually accomplished it, can we?"

"I see," Retsudo answered slowly, "that I must make my meaning clearer. Although they have used sophisticated explosive devices in the past, I am suggesting that a sudden leap into the space age must be viewed with suspicion."

"We . . . are viewing it with suspicion, yes." Kelly recognised Fleming's expression. *Should I tell Oyama about Guiness's suspicions?* He changed the subject. "Under the circumstances, it would seem impossible to meet our deadline, although I think I can guarantee safe delivery of the cable. I hope that this problem will not escalate beyond negotiability?"

"As I said before, Mr. Fleming, we understand terrorists. There are two things to remember in dealing with them. First: we must *never* acceede to their demands. Second: those of us who abhor their actions must be prepared to stand together against them. I know that I speak for my father when I say that Oyama Construction will be willing to make reasonable trade for time and money lost."

"Thank you," Fleming said, desperately wishing he could reach out and shake this man's hand. *He understands, by God!* "Thank you so very much, Retsudo. Unless there is something else, we have work to do."

There was nothing else, and the Japanese signed off, his image evaporating in snow. Fleming's mouth set in a grim line. "Conners, if there is any chance that that explosion didn't originate on Earth . . . "

He didn't need to finish the sentence.

Kelly broke a chilly silence. "Doctor, if it *was* a bomb . . . a mine . . . then surely whoever set it would have left with the rest of the Earthbound?"

Fleming didn't look up. "Yes. We might hope so. There's no way to be sure, not until we check out everyone who had access to *Anansi* during its drydock. Unfortunately, that could be almost anyone."

Thomas nudged the left toggle on his mobility pack, and came in for a closer look at the cable package. The tail was half in black shadow, half in blazing sunlight. The outer shell of foamed lunar stone, man-made pumice, had cracked and splintered, isolating the twisted fins and their attached motors. Thomas caught glimpses of the inner envelope in curves of blackened steel.

It looked unreal. Surrealistic sculpture.

"Thomas?"

"I'm moving in now. Contact in about ten seconds."

"We have you, Thomas. How's the leg?"

"The seal is fine. Hurts, though. I think there's shrapnel buried in there. As long as it hurts I'm not worried. If it starts getting numb I'm coming straight back in."

"Make that a promise. Be careful, there may be another surprise out there."

Thomas looked back at *Anansi*, all highlight and shadow as it hung some four hundred meters away. "Booby trap?" He considered. "It *might* have been a missile. Whatever it was, believe me, I'm not playing hero."

He played the jets as the cable pod approached. His legs took the last few pounds of recoil, and he hovered a few centimeters from the pod. He shone a hand-light into the wound. "Ripped right down to the inner package, but . . . ." For the first time in an hour, a grin broke across his face. "I'll be damned if it doesn't look secure."

"Are you sure?"

"I'll be surer in a minute, but I really think the cable's intact."

"Thank goodness. I—" Marion broke off. When he came back on, all the pleasure in his voice had been leeched out. "Thomas, I'm picking up something on the radar. Two blips, rising through the atmosphere above South America, ahead of us. Hold on, I'm getting Janet up here." Another pause, while Thomas pivoted his mobility pack, found South America and searched the clouds. "Do you have visual contact?"

Another missile! We can't take another hit—
"I don't have anything yet." He drifted away from the cable pod. He strained his eyes, the pain in his leg becoming a thundering heartbeat. "I see something. Two dots."

Janet was back on the line. "I'm here, Tommy. There's two of them. They seem to be matching course with us. What can you see?"

At last he could make something out. Two points of light became finned wedges— "*Not* missiles." Even at that distance, there was no mistaking that shape. "We've got Shuttles here, people."

Marion laughed nervously. "The cavalry arrives."

Janet cut in, totally unamused. "Wait a minute. Who in the world had time to put together a rescue mission? Open hailing frequencies, Marion. Let's see just what we have here."

Thomas watched the ships approach, a tickle of unease growing into a snarled ball of worms in his stomach. He could hear his breathing whistle harshly in his helmet. He tried to relax. It was pointless to speculate until Janet and Marion could talk to the Shuttles . . .

"This is the Space Shuttle *Anansi* calling unidentified Shuttles. Please acknowledge." Marion sat back in his seat and watched the speaker. No answer.

Janet watched the radar image on the cathode ray display, wishing that they had visual contact. "Well, there are any number of possible reasons. Set our receiver to search the bands—they might be using an odd frequency."

He nodded, complying. "About three kilometers now—"

The speaker came to life with a crackle of sound. The voice it carried was American. "*Anansi*. This is the Shuttle *Brasilia*. Do you copy? Over."

"We copy, *Brasilia*. What's your business?"

The man on the other end laughed easily. "We're playing good neighbor. Heard about your trouble and came running."

Marion started to speak, but Janet raised a finger of warning and switched on her own headset. "This is Captain De Camp of *Anansi*. We appreciate the thought. We can use a push, all right. You people are very efficient—

I assume that you put the mission together from scratch in . . . say, three hours?" It was difficult to keep the sarcasm from her voice, but she thought she'd managed it.

Maybe not. The American laughed less easily this time. "Not from scratch. We were preparing for test runs in just under twenty-four hours. When we heard about your problem we had an opportunity to test our emergency procedures. They worked. It was worth it just to find out."

Marion shook his head, made a *thumbs down* sign. Janet snorted silently, but said, "I'll buy that. Who am I speaking to? And why are there two Shuttles? One's enough to tote us down."

Brasilia was silent for about fifteen seconds. Marion said, "They're about two kilometers away now. One of them is slowing to a crawl."

"This is Captain Burgess speaking. We were set for a double launch when the news came in. The other ship is *Willy Ley*. Nobody aboard speaks English."

"Who sponsored the launch?"

There was another pause. "The Brazilian government owns both Shuttles."

Marion said it, softly: "That's not an answer."

Janet asked, "Why weren't we notified that you were coming?"

"We tried to reach you, couldn't get an answer. We assumed that your radio was damaged. Is that the case?"

"That is . . . possible. All right, Brasilia, what's your plan?"

"Depends on your situation. Can you reenter?"

She couldn't avoid a question so simple and so urgent. "No. We can't move. Both of the aft Reaction Control System pods are torn to hell."

"Well, as soon as it can be arranged, we'd like to take you aboard."

"And our cargo?"

Another pause. "We may be able to move your baggage into *Brasilia*'s cargo bay." Burgess' tones were soothing. "You've sustained damage, and it would probably be healthy to come with us. Wasn't there a nuclear plant aboard that ion drive? Falling Angel can send a repair crew, later."

Janet sat back from the board, frowning. "We'll have to think it over."

"Don't take too long. After all, you can't reenter, and you can't return to Falling Angel. We're just trying to help."

"I said—we'll think about it." She turned the radio off. She said, "Salvage."

"Maybe."

"Burgess. Ever hear of him?"

Marion watched the radar blips creeping toward them. "The name rings a bell, but I can't be sure. NASA, I think."

"And renting out to Brazil now?"

"You know something? That stinks." One of

the dots was at rest near the cable pod. The other drifted toward *Anansi*. "The runner-up in the cable bidding was Brazilian. I think we'd better assume that our Captain Burgess is in the employ of Brazil Techimetal-Electromotores. They want the cable."

Janet popped open a squeeze bottle of water and took a swallow's worth. She squinted at the radar screen. "Tommy." She opened the ship-to-suit band and started to speak.

Marion touched the base of her neck, caressingly, and put his lips to her ear. "Be careful. They'll pick up our transmission."

Janet combed her yellow hair with her fingers, fighting light-headedness. Distraction was the last thing she needed. Damned stupid stud! She hadn't been laid in days, and Marion hadn't either, and from the look of him now—concerned, alert, ready to back her up—the thought had never crossed his mind. Perhaps it hadn't. The caress could have been habit . . .

Janet thought cool thoughts. When she was ready, she said, "Tommy? This is *Anansi*. How is everything out there?"

Pause, then a hiss of radio contact. "Just fine. I've got company. About a hundred meters away, just sitting there. I feel very protected. What's the word?"

"Well, it looks like we're out of the woods. All we have to do is hitch a ride and go home."

Please, Tommy—

"That sounds pretty good. I'm getting lonely out here. We'll want to make a pretty thorough damage report before we leave, and we'll have to check out procedure with Falling Angel. Could take a few hours, though, so we'd better get on with it. Oh, by the way—" his voice took on a deceptively casual tone. "The ship here with me is *Brasilia*. The one heading toward you is *Willy Ley*. Didn't the Brazilian government buy that one about five years ago?"

"Go to the front of your class. Our friends are from Brazil."

"Well . . . as long as they don't want to play *piñata* with *Anansi* I guess we'll be all right. I think I'll stay here and check the cable pod awhile longer, if you don't mind."

"How's your air?"

"Fine. I switched bottles when I brought Marion in. By the way. Falling Angel and our Japanese friends both have a legitimate interest in any decisions made out here. Let's tie them into the communications link."

Janet pressed her mike a little closer to her mouth, smiling. "I like that idea. You hang on out there. There's an answer to this."

"Let's define the questions first. Call me when you have something." And he clicked off.

Janet resisted the image of Thomas, tiny against the hulk of the cable pod, sandwiched between it and the Shuttle *Brasilia*. So vulnerable . . .

Marion sensed her mood and laughed aloud. " 'Play *piñata* with *Anansi*.' Was that

Thomas saying that?"

"We're all going to get a little crazy before this is over." *Tommy*... "Listen," she said, forcing her mind back into an analytical set. "We've got two Brazilian Shuttles appearing impossibly fast."

On the radar screen, *Willey Ley* had nearly drawn abreast of *Anansi*. "They only need one to take us down," Marion said. "The other must be for the cable. They can moor to the cable and claim salvage. Might even have equipment to repair the heat shielding." His boyish face darkened. "That's assuming they knew just what kind of damage to expect."

The black underbelly of *Willy Ley* was pulling into their field of vision. Janet watched it speculatively. "They killed Dexter. One ship ... only one ship is doing all the talking. The other one is hanging over our heads, ready for action if things go wrong. 'Jane' back there—" she jerked an impatient thumb in the direction of the cable pod and *Brasilia* —"is going to be all sweetness and light until they realize how much we've figured out."

"Then 'Tarzan' swings in and takes the bananas."

Janet laughed suddenly. "Burgess is cute." She caught Marion staring and said, "Not cute that way. I meant that offer to take what's in the cargo bay down for us. It's all stuff for handling the cable. So the tools go down to Brazil, while *Willy Ley* claims the cable. The BTE offers to buy the tools too."

"Cute," Marion said without a smile. *Willy Ley* had halted, hanging suspended above them, a silent reminder of their helplessness. "We've got to get out of here. There's no way in the world that we can let them get away with this kind of piracy."

"We can't go anywhere. No rocket motors." Janet pounded her fists against the console, hard, once only. "Never mind. If there's a way, I'll find it. We'll find it."

Ten

DRAWING THE LINE

"Tommy. Do you read me?" The sound fought its way through a cloud of pain, a rhythmic pulsing that swirled up Thomas' leg and into his chest. He jumped when he heard the voice. Must have dozed off . . . In panic, he checked his air gauges. No problem. It was just too warm, too quiet and, with his face-plate fully polarized, too dark. Sleep was a natural path for a body in pain to take.

He looked up, saw *Willy Ley* blotting out the stars like a great dark scavenger, its belly armored with heat-shield scales. "I'm here." His breath whistled in his ears. "My friend is here too." He rotated his suit to face *Anansi*. She seemed close enough to reach out and touch, a toy floating at arm's length. "I'd really like to come home."

"How's the leg?"

"It still hurts, so it's okay, I guess." The patch on his knee was secure, but it was too easy to picture torn flesh under it, and he winced away from the image.

Janet sounded relieved. "Good. Listen. We're thinking about the ride home we've been offered—"

No! "Janet, listen—"

She interrupted him urgently. "No, Thomas, *you* listen. We have to remember what Dr. Anansi always said: 'You have to know where to draw the line.'"

Dr. Anansi? What the hell was she talking about?

"So check over the pod once more, then come on back. No arguments—I hope I don't have to make myself any clearer."

Thomas thought furiously. She was afraid the bandits might eavesdrop. Reasonable. So: *Dr. Anansi.* Doctor Shuttle? Doctor Spider? The Shuttle was named for an archetypal spider, a nasty character from African legend who had crept into Heaven and been evicted. *Draw the line?* It hit him suddenly, and he grinned into his microphone. "I'll be heading back in a few minutes. I've only got a little *moor* to do out here."

He hoped she'd caught it.

"Fine, Tommy. We'll be waiting to hear from you."

Thomas sipped from the nipple at his cheek and washed his mouth out hard before swallowing. It wasn't cold, but it helped him feel awake and alive. His battery gauge looked okay; he turned up his cooling system a little. He detached his safety line and crawled back along the gently curved surface of the cable pod.

It was clear enough what she wanted ... and that wasn't going to be easy. But for what?

There were steel handholds and foot rests placed for the benefit of those who had built the cable pod. Thomas was glad for that. Early astronauts had half killed themselves trying to work in free fall with nothing to brace themselves.

Anansi = spider. Doctor = Dexter Stonecypher. Draw the line—

Thomas paused, gripping one of the metal hand rungs. *They killed Dexter!* The thought echoed within his skull, a mix of grief and incredulity and rage, shockingly strong. Thomas wasn't used to dealing with rage.

He moved on. *Willey Ley* was a massive shadowed wedge: like an Empire battleship from *Star Wars*, ludicrously dangerous.

Access to the cable was at the back of the pod, between the fins. Heat from the explosion had remelted some of the lunar slag, and Thomas' fears were justified: the access plug, a steel screw-hatch set in the cannister and now showing through the ripped foam shell, was warped. He crawled closer, splaying his feet out to find the foot rests set into the shell. One was partly burned away, and he took a moment to wedge his toe under the remnant, a twisted steel loop.

He gripped the wheel-shaped handle and turned as powerfully as he could, straining until it felt like his shoulders were coming apart. He felt his fingers biting into the glove padding, felt his leg wound start to burn. The wheel didn't budge.

Thomas detached the cable gripper from his belt. It was a great clumsy plier-like thing with blades and pressure points of tungsten carbide, designed solely for gripping or cutting Stonecypher's cable. The enormous gear ratios and the small motors inside it made it a massive object indeed.

It made a dandy hammer. He braced himself and pounded the wheel a few times, rim and center. *Break up the vacuum cementing.* He tried the wheel again. It didn't move.

He flipped on his radio. "Janet. There's something here that needs to be secured, or vice versa, but my air will be running low in about fifteen minutes. I may have to leave it."

"Your choice."

Thomas detached the cutting torch from his belt. He braced himself anew, for fear of being jarred loose. In free fall and vacuum, the torch would act as a rocket. It even had a flared nozzle to direct most of the flaming gas away from the man holding it . . . and some of it still sprayed in all directions into the hard vacuum.

He worked the torch in a circle around the screw, holding it a fair distance from the metal. He wasn't trying to cut anything, yet. He only wanted to heat the surface as evenly as possible, to expand the metal.

Without atmosphere, there is no convection to help get rid of waste heat. But there *is* conduction, and Thomas, enveloped in gas that was vacuum-thin but flame-hot, was swimming in sweat within a few minutes. Combined with the throbbing in his leg it became almost too much to tolerate. *You can't make it in time*, an insidious voice whispered. *Quit before you damage something. Go back now, try again later.*

"There might not *be* a later!"

"Tommy? Did you say something?"

"Just a little debate with himself. Don't worry, I'm winning."

There was silence on the other end. Then, "Tommy? Are you all right?"

"Fine. I'm just fine." His oxygen was low; the power in his batteries was dropping. He had to try *now*. Another five minutes and he wouldn't have the safety margin he'd need to return to the ship. He clicked off the torch and reached for the wheel.

It was unpleasantly hot, and he knew that without his gloves the flesh of his hands would have been seared to the bone. Again, he set his feet, inhaled deeply, and threw his body into the effort. There was an inch of give, then it stuck again. This time he didn't give up. Thomas gulped another lungful of air, then hissed it out in an explosion of total commitment.

It moved. Sluggishly, as if the screw didn't quite fit the grooves any more, but it moved, and the ion tech grinned in savage satisfaction. Even the *pain* felt good.

He unwound a foot and a half of steel screw before it finally came free. The first two meters of cable were sheathed in yellow plastic a quarter of an inch thick, but after that it seemed to disappear. He cautiously grasped the plastic section and pulled it out into unfiltered sunlight. It unreeled easily.

Beyond the plastic was naked cable, the precious end product of seven years of work and hope. Almost as thin as spider silk, it was a dim hairline that barely reflected the light at all. But frail as it looked, Thomas knew that no man alive could sunder that line with strength alone. He was looking at a miracle of will and patience, and the sight of it helped cool the fire chewing at his nerves.

The yellow plastic was wound around a hook on the underside of the screw and he undid it, sliding out the thin metal bar where the plastic terminated. He tied the bar to his safety line.

His cooling unit hissed, still shedding heat he'd picked up from the welding torch.

He triggered the backpack jets. They took him up and out, and the cable line tautened behind him. Drag slowed him almost to a halt.

But the cable was running free, unwinding, spinning out behind him like a single strand of spider silk. He fired the jets again. *Anansi* wasn't far: a quarter of a mile, no more. If the drag cost him his backpack fuel, the cutting torch would still serve as a rocket.

Thomas loved open spaces. He had traded the vast plains and rugged mountains of his youth in southern Alaska, for a greater vastness. But now, crossing on invisible thread between the cable pod and his own ruined spacecraft, with bandit ships ahead and behind . . . he felt utterly vulnerable. *Can't fight, can't run. Has Janet got something in mind? Or is she just thrashing around?*

For all of his life Thomas had analyzed his emotions and fragmented them and shoved them away into convenient pockets. Later he could take them out, like moldy, forgotten, half-melted candy bars, and examine those old feelings after they were too dead to hurt him. He knew that was what he would be doing in the asteroids. Safely distant from Janet and a ruined marriage, he would exhume the memories and perform an intellectual autopsy. Probing here, culturing there, until he knew everything about it that there was to know, and could file it away forever.

And never, never experience it.

But he was tired and frightened, and there was too much room to feel his insignificance, his knowledge and accomplishments and goals fading into dreams. His reality was the vastness around him and the slow, ragged sound of his own breathing.

The doors of the Shuttle bay were wide with welcome. A pressure-suited shape waved him down. Thomas detached the yellow leader from his safety line, and moored it to a supporting rib on the inside of the bay. He said, "The mobility unit's dead."

"I'll refuel it now."

"Bombs," Thomas said. "Time or radio controlled. If they put one in the locking ring, maybe—"

"I searched." Marion shook his head. "Can't find anything that shouldn't be there, but there's no way to search everything. You want to open every package in the cargo bay?"

"No."

Janet spoke in their helmets. "Marion, are you ready to go for the limpet motors? We've got to have them."

"I'll go right after I refuel the mobility unit."

"What's chances of their spotting you?"

Marion grinned. "Oh, they will, but they're not likely to guess what I'm doing."

As he dream-walked to the airlock, Thomas saw Dexter Stonecypher's two-meters-plus of pressure suit lashed to the side of the cargo bay, partially wrapped in tarps. It looked almost like a clumsily prepared mummy, but for the ridged boots sticking out at the lower edge. He stepped into the lock, still looking back at his friend's body.

Air hissed in. Thomas unscrewed his helmet and ran the back of a gloved hand over his face. He was sweat-sticky and knew that his dark eyes were puffy.

The inner lock opened. Janet was in the lower deck, scribbling on paper stretched up against the lockers. Thomas said, "Hi. Why do we need limpet motors?"

"In a minute, Tommy." She turned from her paperwork. "Let's look at your leg."

Thomas was exhausted on every level his senses could touch, but still felt himself tense when Janet began helping him out of his suit. "I can do it, damnit—" he started to say, and only then realized how his voice and body were trembling.

"Don't, Tommy. Don't push me away now, please? You need help. Don't make me pull rank on you."

Somehow, that made him smile. He stumbled back out of his suit, limbs feeling clumsy and swollen. He hadn't noticed it before, but his left leg didn't hurt as much anymore.

There was blood darkening the synthetic material of his overalls, partially clotted now, and he didn't resist as Janet helped him to a web. He curled his fingers around its strands and closed his eyes. He heard her busy herself at the first aid cabinet, felt her as she snipped away the material to expose the wound.

"Tommy . . . you should have let Marion do the inspection. This should have gotten attention hours ago."

He felt too weak to argue, and didn't. Her hands were cool and soothing as they manipulated his leg, gently wiped away the thickened blood. "There's something in there, all right. This is going to hurt a little." He flinched as the knifepoint of pain lanced into the muscle over his knee. Thomas heard his wife's words of encouragement as if they were whispered far away.

"There," she said, and he opened his eyes. She stood, holding a shard of grayish shrapnel between the tips of her surgical tweezers. He teased it away from her and turned it over in his fingers. "Foamed ceramic," she said. "Part of the cable pod."

She dressed his wound, and held his hand as he flexed the leg experimentally. "I think it will work," he said, wincing. "Thank you." Their eyes met, and he knew that some of the accumulated resistance was gone, that a direct current of understanding passed between them. His mouth grew cottony, and he swallowed hard. "I'm tired, Janet, but I can keep going. Now. Why did you want the cable? And why the limpet motors?"

"I've got an idea." She waved at the expanse of scribble-covered paper. "Look it over. Tell me if I'm crazy."

Glad that there was no gravity to test his knee, Thomas crossed to stare at her diagrams.

She had sketched a Shuttle outline, recognizably *Anansi*. A line ran straight up from the Shuttle's open cargo doors. An arc of Earth's surface was below. The line reached up to a rocklike shape with fins. In the middle of the line were the words "Approx 2 km?". Off to the side were two *Anansi*-shaped craft emblazoned with skull and crossbones.

"I'll be damned. Tides," he said.

Janet spoke from behind him. In her voice was a touch of belligerence, and a bit of a stammer too. "After all, we want *Anansi* to go *down*, right? And the cable should go *up*, out of their reach. Well?"

"You're not much of an artist," he said, images flowing together in his mind like colors in a paint-by-numbers drawing. "But you don't have to be. You're one hell of a smart lady."

"Will it work? *Anansi* can stand a re-entry, right? The heat shielding is almost intact. Maybe some of the tail would burn away, but—"

He waved it away. "That's your department. If you think we can re-enter, fine. Getting down is the problem. We don't have any rockets, barring the nose jets and . . . even one limpet motor would do it, this way, except that it'd take longer."

"Okay. And the bandits are the original Shuttles. That design was proxmired in the seventies. Congress tried to build it cheap, and it doesn't carry enough fuel to get very high. If we can put the cable in a higher orbit, it'll be out of their reach. They'd have to launch a Shuttle with an auxiliary tank. Falling Angel will have an ion tug here before they could launch. I think we can beat them," she said, moving up close behind him. She seemed a little breathless. "The cable can take the stress if *Anansi* can."

"*Anansi* and the cable and Dexter's special staples and glue. It *all* has to hold. Mmm . . ."

Enveloping the squat outline of the Shuttle were wavy lines representing atmosphere, above the curve of the Earth's surface. In Thomas's mind, stress vectors performed a wardance, and he burned to get to his computer. "Nobody's ever tried anything like this," he said slowly, "except for some early gravity-stabilized camera satellites. The satellites would reel wires out in opposite directions, and tidal effect held the wires oriented on a line through the Earth. They don't do that any more."

"Why not?"

"There are better ways to stabilize a satellite. Never mind. We have all the information in the world on the cable, the structural strength of *Anansi*, tidal stress, winds . . ." his voice trailed off. "I'll have to try to program a model of this."

"Marion and I tried it, but you'd better check us out."

"I'll do my own." The excitement was building up inside him, its brightness pushing aside the waves of uncertainty and fatigue, and he knew, even before he checked it with the computer, that Janet had found a way out.

Marion cycled through the airlock, pulling off his helmet. "Two limpet motors, no obvious damage. I moored them in the bay. How's it look, Thomas?"

"I can't tell yet. What about the Brazilian Shuttles?" Thomas ran a dark finger along the pencil line connecting Shuttle and cannister. "They may not sit back and let us rescue ourselves."

Marion floated up behind him. He was puffing. "Listen, Thomas—it's not quite as bad as that. The bandits can't even *see* the cable. We use those last limpet motors to thrust us down and backward in our orbit. They'll see that, but they won't know why. Down and back puts us in a lower orbit than the cable pod. We'll pull ahead of the cable pod before the line goes taut. When the cable starts reeling out, maybe they'll figure out what we're doing." His smile, still tinged with darkness, began to glow with the promise of merry Hell. "By that time it'll be too late to grab the cannister or stop us. *Let* them try to match orbits with us! We won't be *in* an orbit!"

"We'll have to stall them somehow," Thomas mused, thoughts snaking away in a dozen directions at once. "We can't be sure how desperate they are."

"Sure we can." Janet tapped a long finger

hard on one of the Jolly Rogers. "This is the first act of space-age piracy. It takes a lot of momentum to get a ball like this rolling. BTE must have its ass right on the line. Hundreds of millions at stake. With that kind of motivation, their contingency plans are bound to include murder."

"They've proved that already. Thomas, *Willy Ley* hasn't said word one the whole time it's been over our heads. *Brasilia* says that *Ley*'s pilots don't speak English." Marion snorted. "That's bullshit. Everyone who flies speaks English; it's the international language in that sense. I don't think they really expect us to swallow their story without chewing it. They think they have us in a total bind. It's a psychological pressure play, with a lie just thick enough to give us an honorable way out. If we don't respond, they go to Plan Two—which might well be blowing us right out of the sky."

A flash of his distorted dream, a dream of screaming steel that flamed from the sky . . . "All right," Thomas said. "How do we handle it? Janet?"

"I'll handle the communications. If there are any questions from 'Jane'—" she ruffled her blond hair ruefully. "—*Brasilia*, I'll be ready to answer them. We also need to keep up some harmless chatter with Falling Angel and Oyama. Harmless chatter." The words seemed to choke her. "God, I hate this. I want so *bad* to tell those bastards exactly what I think of them, and here I have to chit-chat like Sunday supper."

"Let's get to work, then." Thomas moved to a computer input. His fingers were twitching. "None of us is going to feel alive until we're *doing* something. And I don't think you have to worry about the 'harmless chatter.' They know we're upset. They won't expect frivolity. Show you're hurt. Hide the anger."

Janet nodded. "As long as they know. Eventually."

Eleven

IN PLAIN VIEW

Half the boxes and pressure-packed equipment in the cargo bay had to be moved, restacked and lashed to the walls to redistribute the floor space. Although weightless, the cargo had considerable mass, and it was work to move it, to brace properly against the velcro traction strips or support struts. Inertia must always be reckoned with.

They walked wide around the cable, which reached straight up into the black sky from where Thomas had anchored the yellow leader.

Likewise they avoided the silent, motionless cocoon of Dexter Stonecypher. Thomas found it difficult not to hear the metallurgist's voice in his ears, to feel the dead gaze on the nape of his neck. When he moved crated cutting tools,

Stonecypher was there urging caution. The cable grippers and special gloves were boxed separately, and had to be moved to the side. Without them, the cable was nearly useless, capable of slicing through the strongest case-hardened metals like a razor through skin. Yet they were not just tools, they were Dexter's legacy, and there was a nearly reverential silence as they worked.

When they were finished, the walls of the entire bay were lined and stacked with boxes, but most of the floorspace was clear.

Marion removed a cable gripper from the already opened package, and worked it a few times to lubricate the joints. With his feet anchored in Velcro, he reached up and clamped the tool to the cable. He pulled it to the floor. It gave easily, and sprang back. The quarter-mile length was too flexible.

"We need slack, and we can't pull it out from here," Marion said with some reluctance. "It won't unreel. We'd end up with the whole cable pod nestling cosily up against us."

"Okay."

Marion saw Thomas unloading a fresh mobility pack. "Hold it. Isn't that my job now? You're hurt."

"Pulling cable out is the easy part. You'll be here doing the muscle work."

Marion digested that. "We need a couple of kilometers of slack. Thomas, you'll have all that cable hanging loose around you, and it's damn near invisible, and it cuts *anything*."

Thomas had worked himself into the mobility pack. "There's that too. *Gabriel*'s out of action, and I can't fly the Shuttle. Which of us is expendable? Janet could pull rank here, but we don't really want to ask her, do we?"

Marion laughed unconvincingly. "I didn't know you were tactful, Thomas. All right, go."

Thomas rose in a nearly invisible burst of thrusters. Marion turned back to work. He had opened a crate of Stonecypher's special staples when he heard, "Marion?"

"Here, Janet."

"Any problems?"

"Nothing we can't handle." Did she know where Thomas had gone?

"I want you to hook a camera to the manipulator arm. I want to maintain visual contact at all times."

He couldn't help glancing up at the hovering black wedges. A picture of silent, armed figures emerging from *Brasilia*'s open cargo doors, gliding down to *Anansi*—"I'll do that now."

He hooked the auxiliary camera up, and tied it into the main video display. "Are you getting it?"

"Fine." She didn't ask where Thomas was. So far their words had given nothing away, painted no image save that of a desperate Shuttle crew trying to save what they could of their mission.

Videoscreen #3, directly to Janet's right and below the rectangle of the Surface Position Indicator, filled with snow as the camera activated. She waited for the automatic tuning to do its best before she began to fiddle.

The manipulator arm, its eight-meter lengths jointed skeletally, rose into the open. The rear third of *Anansi* came into view. The sight of the ruined RCS pods tightened her chest. The left was shredded, the right peppered with shrapnel holes: fine machinery, brutally mangled. At her command the camera tilted back down toward the cargo bay.

Marion looked up at the camera. "We're ready here, Janet. How's the picture?"

"Prime time. Let me check the rotation." She rolled the camera until she was looking past one of the bay doors, down toward the blue mists of Earth and the silent "Tarzan," *Willey Ley*. She toyed with the thought of trying to talk to them again, then directed the camera back down into the bay. "Everything's fine. Color's fine. Carry on."

Marion began setting staples. Janet rotated the camera until she was looking *up*: out of the bay, outward from Earth. Tommy was a dwarfed, shapeless figure approaching a great grey monolith, the cable pod.

At a thousand kilometers distance, in full sunlight, Earth was big enough to spark the fear of falling. Thomas' jets pushed him outward, past one black wedge-shaped bandit and toward another.

They'd see everything. The tail of the cable pod was in full sunlight; *Anansi*'s cargo bay yawned wide open. They'd see, but would they understand?

Thomas came in slowly, to one side of the ruined tail. The cable was a thread of light, glowing in raw sunlight, easy to avoid as he pulled himself around the jagged shards of torn heat-shielding.

Thomas set grippers to the cable, tugging gingerly at first, then with increasing power. After a moment's hesitation it began to unwind from the spool. He pulled it out a meter at a time. At first the line remained almost taut; then it began to form loops.

The staples were pencil-thin in the center: tungsten carbide with a core of the cable itself, splaying out into two broad pads of hard steel alloy. Marion mounted them close together, fixing them to the deck with the epoxy gun. The epoxy would take thirty seconds to set.

He had twenty staples in place, in two rows, and the cable was slack now, hanging in curves. He began stringing the cable. The special gloves fit well enough over his pressure suit gloves, but he was leery of using them. He kept his hands on the yellow leader, stringing it under the staples. Then he sprayed the three lengths with more of Stonecypher's special epoxy.

The staple box was half empty. Marion pursed his lips. Then he began laying more cable, continuing the zigzag pattern. He used cable grippers to hold the strands in place while he sprayed epoxy down its length.

He could feel the strain of exertion in his back, and his suit was getting warm. Good warmup, this. Finish with stretching exercises . . . in an hour or two, or three. Thomas had given him plenty of slack, and he could think of no excuse for stopping. Twenty strands . . . thirty . . . no more sunlight now. The floods in the cargo bay gave plenty of light. He'd lay a hundred strands or so, and plant staples along the last three.

Don't get too tired, he told himself. *Tired people make mistakes, and this stuff is deadly. Wup! Thomas doesn't have any light at all!*

"Thomas, Marion speaking. I've got enough to work with. Take a break. Wait for dawn before you start again," he said, hoping that was cryptic enough for the bandit ships. Hoping Janet could spin them a song and dance . . . but lying was not one of Janet's skills, Marion thought. A few good lies might have saved her marriage. She'd have to learn quick, to save the cable.

Enough of Stonecypher's epoxy and special staples might be enough to hold Stonecypher's cable. They might rip up some of the floor, too, but *Anansi* was a wreck already. Just one more re-entry, and then the Shuttle would be junk. Or ionized vapor.

Dawn touched the cable first, a thread of light leading down toward Earth and *Anansi*. The curves were straightening out. Marion must have been working hard, Thomas thought.

He set back to pulling cable. His abused arm and shoulder muscles had stiffened, and he groaned and kept working. The cable hung in loops around him.

It would have to do, Marion thought. He was getting too far aft in the cargo bay. It wouldn't do to have *Anansi* hanging nose down. Besides . . . if he laid twice that much cable it would give them no more safety at all. It would hold or it wouldn't.

He took a break. No need to lie "down"; he simply closed his eyes and let every separate muscle relax. A minute passed, or two, or five . . .

To work. Marion removed the two remaining limpet motors from their clamps and plugged them in for a diagnostic. "Janet?"

"Everything seems fine, Marion."

"Good. Tommy, you've probably done enough out there. Come on back. I can use some help here."

Thomas was puffing. "I can use a change. Coming in."

The men had both taken a few minutes' rest,

and Janet was glad. They were working too hard. Now, too soon, she watched Thomas trigger his backpack and come straight up toward the camera, hauling the pair of limpets after him.

A quick flutter of fingertips and she had the medical readouts on screen #1. She checked his heartbeat and respiration. Safe, but still too high. She could still hear his voice as he swore at her: *Dammit, if there's any risk involved, I have to be the one to take it. I am expendable. You and Marion are not.*

From the mission's perspective he was right, of course, but that didn't make it easier. He seemed almost frantic with energy. He spoke with too much emotion, too much spon- teneity, and it was a little frightening. *Or is it? Isn't that what you always wanted . . .?*

Not a comfortable thought. Worse: was her husband trying to out-macho Marion? It would be utterly unlike him . . . but what in God's name would she *do* about it?

The camera followed Thomas toward *Anansi's* tail, limpet motors trailing behind him like fishing bobbers floating in a dark- ened sea.

The intercom hissed. "This shouldn't be too bad, but I wish we didn't have to depend on the limpets."

"What's on your mind, Tommy?"

"Control. We can control the forward atti- tude jets more precisely than we can control these."

She shrugged into the blind microphone. "They don't have enough fuel. We've got the limpets lined up along the original motors. They should thrust through the Shuttle's center of mass. If they're off a little, I've still got the nose jets."

The ship-to-ship line broke in, and the voice on the other end was curiously polite. "This is *Brasilia* calling *Anansi*." Janet turned the camera to get a good look at *Brasilia* hovering just beyond the cable pod.

"Captain De Camp here, Burgess. What can I do for you?" She kept her voice as light as possible.

He fumbled for the thought. "Ah . . . we see that you've gone EVA . . . apparently affecting repairs—"

What sharp little eyes you have, you bastard.
"Yes. That's exactly what we're doing."

Another pause. Then, "Can we be of assistance?"

Could they see into the Shuttle bay? And if they could, could they possibly see the zigzags of cable and guess their purpose? Not likely, but the suspicion in Burgess' voice called for careful judgment. "I can't think of anything we can't do for ourselves. What did you have in mind?"

"Captain De Camp, if I'm talking out of turn, so be it. We can see you placing limpet motors on what's left of your RCSPs. Now, you've *got* to know that two limpet motors won't change your orbit by more than a hundred kilometers or so—"

"Less."

"Even if you could reach atmosphere... well, your ship doesn't look like it can still maneuver. If you accept our offer and let us take you down—"

So you can claim Shuttle, cable, everything in our cargo bay and what's left of the ion drive too? "No, we have to try this. But if it doesn't work we'll be glad to accept your offer."

Pause. "We may not be able to wait forever. Why not be reasonable?"

The first glint of steel beneath the glove? "Burgess, you have to understand. We may have lost the cable and the ion drive—" she knew he would love hearing *that*—"but we've got to try to save what we can. Leave us that much dignity, please."

She swivelled the camera, searching for Thomas. He had reached the left RCSP, and was adjusting the limpet before triggering its magnetic lock. Behind and above him, *Brasilia* seemed to have drifted closer. She hoped it was an illusion.

"Burgess... how much room do you have aboard?"

"Three crew, seven seats. Plenty of room for you. We were prepared for guests, but we heard about your casualty." She was surprised to hear unmistakable sincerity in the man's next words: "Dr. Stonecypher was a great man."

"Yes . . . yes, he was." She was puzzled now. She tried to keep the emotion from building, but it was there in her voice. *It's all right, they expect you to be upset about Dexter, don't they?* "He was easy to care about. Half-crazy sometimes, maybe. But I guess you can't be a seven-foot-tall genius and not be . . ." *That's too much. These people killed Dexter!*

There was no sound from the other end of the line, but she knew that Burgess was listening, and that *Willy Ley* was listening too. The next words were for them. "When you're in a tightly-knit community like Falling Angel, eccentrism just breaks the monotony. You care about those people—it's hard not to. They're likely to be the most straightforward, dedicated, intelligent people you'll ever meet in your life. You tend to make them family. Brothers, sisters . . . and if Fleming is Falling Angel's father, then Dexter Stonecypher was our uncle, the crazy one nobody understands and everybody loves.

"Now he's dead. Terrorists killed him. The United Muslim Activist Front, I believe they said. They killed him, and someone is going to pay for that." She was trembling, and paused to relax her stranglehold on the control panel.

Burgess spoke slowly. "I see what you're saying, yes."

"I hope so. After all, you're part of this too, aren't you?"

Silence. Then, "What do you mean?"

"Space. 'The Final Frontier.' How much of

your life have you invested in it? You must
have dreamed the same dreams as Fleming
and Stonecypher, and me. You must have
watched '2001' and 'Star Trek', and read the
books, and listened to the same people sing
the same songs. And watched the sky. You had
to.''

There was no answer from the other side,
only the faint sound of breathing. *By God!
What kind of pirate is this? The man feels
something!* The current was flowing now. En-
couraged, she continued, working the hook in
a little deeper. ''So when something threatens
that dream, when maniacs attack us to shore
up their rickety ideology, or even worse—''
she wished she could see Burgess' face, to
know exactly how far she was twisting the
knife. ''Or even worse, for *money*, well, friend,
that's tearing at the heart of the dream, that
hurts *me*, because I give a damn. I hope you
can say the same thing.'' She leaned back
from the microphone, drunken with the need
to vent her anger.

''What the hell else would we be doing
here?'' Burgess asked with answering anger.
''Do you know what one Shuttle launch
costs?''

Thomas' voice broke in. ''I've got the
limpets set up, Janet. We're ready for a test
firing.''

''Good, Tommy. Get back into the bay and
secure.''

Burgess spoke. ''*Anansi*— I'm still not sure

what it is you have planned . . ."

"You don't have to be," she said bluntly. "We're going home, if we can. If we can't, we'll lock up *Anansi* and come down with you. Fair enough?"

She armed the limpets through the main computer and synchronized them with the forward attitude jets. She triggered the vernier thrusters. The blue-white globe below the wings rolled forward, until the cabin windows looked straight down on Borneo and Sumatra.

She hoped Tommy had given her *lots* of slack on the cable. Without that the cable could slice deep into *Anansi*. She couldn't ask, not by intercom . . . She let *Anansi* roll a few degrees further. Then a short burst of verniers slowed and stabilized the Shuttle, pointing down-and-backward in its orbit.

Down and back puts us in a lower, faster orbit than the cable pod. We'll pull ahead before the line goes taut. The cable pod pulls Anansi *backward; we slow; we drop. Anansi pulls the cable pod forward; it speeds up; it rises. Will it work? Tommy says it'll work.*

Above and behind her were the cable pod, and *Wiley Ley*. She moved the manipulator arm to peek over the damaged RCS pods, and found them.

"Beautiful so far," Tommy said happily. "I think we're ready for a test firing."

"Are you secure?"

"We're both in the bay, tied down."

"In five." She counted off the seconds and started the limpets. The thrust built up behind her: trivial pressure, just enough to disturb her semicircular canals. She kept an eye on *Brasilia*, waiting, then sighed as the bandit Shuttle began to inch past.

They had never planned a test firing. To what point? They didn't have fuel to spare. She had expected Burgess to be shouting at her by now, but there wasn't a sound from *Brasilia*. Perhaps he didn't want to interrupt her during a difficult maneuver. Or he might be just confused.

Who *was* Burgess? Why didn't he have the good grace to be smoother, slicker, more like the pirate he had to be?

Anansi was yawing left. The limpet motors weren't quite balanced. Janet used verniers to steady the nose. Vernier fuel wouldn't last forever either . . .

Her camera showed *Willy Ley* and *Brasilia* and the cable pod dwindling aft. *Anansi* lurched as a limpet motor ran dry, and Janet chewed her lip and rode the verniers until the other quit too.

Then, in haste: a long blast of vernier jets to bring the nose away from Earth. When Stonecypher's cable went taut it must stand straight up from the cargo bay. Otherwise it would wrap around the hull and slice away pieces.

Done. "Done! Tommy, Marion, come on back in. We've got work to do," she said, teeth bared in satisfaction.

Twelve

LOOSE ENDS

The sun had set only an hour earlier, but on that camouflaged section of the Iranian plateau, work was nearly completed. Electronic and mechanical equipment, scaffolding, transportation gear and prefabricated living quarters had been broken down and shipped or destroyed.

Djalma Costa watched the last of the half-tracks, sagging with gear, roll groaning into the darkness. Most of the technicians supplied by BTE had already left. Soon there would be little but packed sand and sun-scorched brush, and nothing at all to connect BTE with the historic events of the past twelve hours.

The Prometheus had risen on a billowing cloud of fire and dust. Forty pairs of eyes watched it go, a spontaneous scream of victory urging the missile on. Just as reflexive was Costa's sexual arousal, and his urgent need to retire from the launch site. *They'd launched late, late!*

Never had he experienced anything to compare with that moment. It still flashed to mind as he wove between the evacuating workers, heading back to his own tent. Dark stains glued his shirt to his body, as they had during much of the day. But now the stains were beginning to stink of fear.

They were watching him. There was death in the breeze that flowed across the sand, fluttering canvas and paper, sending dust-imps dancing through the camp.

What did they think of the news report? The "two missile" hypothesis? He remembered Mansur's skeletal face creasing in a thin, inquisitive smile. The explosives expert sat beside the camp radio, sometimes looking at Costa, sometimes back at Hoveida and the bodyguard. In four languages, news broadcasts spoke of the disaster in space . . . and of a missile that must have exploded hundreds of kilometers short.

And in Arabic, his UMAF co-conspirators talked among themselves. At last Hoveida twisted in his canvas chair, his massive body wringing a tortured creak from its frame. "It seems," the terrorist leader said, as calm as Death, "that the missile did not strike the Shuttle squarely."

"I don't understand." Costa held himself to balanced proportions of concern, surprise, consternation. Anything else would be suicide.

Hoveida pivoted the folding chair to watch Costa more carefully. There was no tension in the Arab's body; he was as relaxed as a coiled snake. "I mean that there was an explosion, and the ship was crippled. One crew member was killed, or has died, it is difficult to be sure how this happened. The crew is presently evaluating the damage."

"I . . . I was assured that a strike by a Prometheus was impossible to survive." He let anger seep into expression and body motion, springing from his chair. "I'll have to answer for this—No. At least I'm not responsible for the choice of missile. I proceeded just as instructed." He calmed himself and addressed them apologetically. "Please, I do realize that the fault lay with our equipment, not in the work and planning your people put into the project. Now, how badly *did* we damage them? Spacecraft are so vulnerable. An injured spacecraft should be useless for anything." He *should* want to know these things. Shouldn't he?

He faced Hoveida squarely. *Why doesn't he mention the broadcasts? The cable vehicle might have started down before the Prometheus arrived*, he thought in bitter despair, *so Xavier's men set the bomb off early. Did they give one thought to me?* He saw nothing but questions and coldness in Hoveida. The Arab spoke thickly. "I want no more words. Please go and supervise the withdrawal phase. Mansur and I have much to speak of."

Heading back to his quarters now. The withdrawal was nearly complete, the background noises and sights had faded to a blur against the growing awareness of danger.

Mansur's smile, terrible as the final rictus of some dying animal, played in his mind. They knew they'd been used! The UMAF as a tool of the capitalists . . . how far would their credibility sink if *that* were known? Indeed, mightn't their own followers turn on Hoveida and his Angel of Death?

If they were positive they had been lied to . . . then all of the promised funds would mean nothing, would be no protection at all for BTE's personnel liaison . . . Would Hoveida have to be positive?

Costa was jarred out of his reverie by a scream of rage, and he threw himself backward, stumbling, as a jeep nearly ran him down. The driver shook his fist, spitting worlds in Arabic as he wove his way out of camp. Costa sat on the ground, listening to his attempts to swallow. Dust and fear clogged his throat, making it difficult to breathe.

One of his technicians offered a hand up, and Costa refused, shaking his head violently. The little man dusted himself off and stood, for an instant unsure of his next move. Then, sucking the back of a skinned hand, he headed toward his tent. It rattled its flaps at him as he ducked in, looking back over his shoulder to see if anyone had followed. The camp was an anthill of activity, workers scrambling to a hundred tasks, but there was no sign that he had been singled out.

His luggage lay packed, two cases on his bed, one by the tiny washbasin. Costa opened one of the cases, ran his hands over the contents, afraid to turn on the light. When he found the rectangular shape of the electric shaver he gasped in relief. He turned it over to get at the battery pack. He plugged the auxiliary extension cord in, stretched it out at arm's length, and pushed the "recharge" button. The light at the base of the shaver glowed red, and he knew that the radio signal had been sent. After ten seconds it faded, and he pushed it again, waited, then repacked the shaver. It was a shame to lose it, and the rest of his luggage too, but his only hope lay in moving as quickly as possible.

Costa steadied his nerves, and left the tent.

Leaving the camp was a nightmare, even under cover of darkness. He was sure that every eye followed him, that his every movement was a lethal betrayal. He tried to blend into the shadows, to become part of the night, slipping away from the lights and movement, belly-crawling through the dust and sand until he was far enough from the camp to stand and run.

And run he did, northward, feet slipping on the sand until he felt like a mouse on a treadmill, until he found the patch of hard flat sand he had scouted three nights ago. There, almost a kilometer from the camp and the men he had betrayed, he sat to wait for the helicopter.

There were insect sounds, and the distant purr of motors and voices, but Costa screened those out, peering into the sky, waiting and praying. Where was it? Surely it would come.

Minutes passed. He looked at the glowing face of his watch, and shivered, lying close to the sand. The wind blew coarse grains into his nose, his eyes and mouth, but he lay as silent as a lizard, waiting.

Where was it? Surely the helicopter had been waiting, fueled, pilots at the alert? Surely Xavier had chosen only men who could be trusted with a task of such urgency? Surely Xavier—

A finger of doubt traced its way up his spine, whispering betrayal in his ear. What if Xavier *knew* that he was likely to lose his Liaison officer? *What if you are expendable now, Costa? After all, your part of the job is over . . .*

"No," he said, almost deprecatingly, and shut his eyes tight. That kind of thinking was pure paranoia. Xavier wasn't that kind of man . . .

Then what kind of man was he? Why should he care about Costa now? Costa, the only personal link between the terrorists and BTE . . .

Costa heard the first whimper break from his throat, dying away at the distant sound of helicopter blades cut through the darkness. Relief rolled over him like a freezing breaker, restoring the calm and sanity, sending the doubt scurrying for cover.

He could even see the landing lights. He stood and waved, knowing that they were picking him up on infra-red by now. "Thank God," he said with unaccustomed reverence. "If—"

Something hit him a smashing blow across the back of the head, and he fell, mind too full of sudden pain for questions or even fear to reach him. He fell face down, unable to soften his descent, nose impacting squarely with the sand. It felt broken, clogged with sand and what tasted like blood. A rough hand clamped brutally on his shoulder and rolled him over.

Hoveida planted a knee squarely on Costa's right arm, put the point of his knife over the little man's solar plexus. His eyes gleamed in the dim light. "We will find your master, never fear, and will send him to join you in Hell."

Costa tried to speak, but as he opened his mouth something slid into his body, tearing his body, tearing his vitals, and the breath to speak or scream was pinned within him. Hoveida smiled broadly, pulled the knife free and wiped its blade on Costa's face.

From the corner of his eye Costa saw the helicopter draw nearer, heard shots. With a sudden whine of the engines, the copter veered away, climbing into the sky. "No," Costa said, or thought he said. Don't leave me. The copter seemed to respond, sinking toward the sand; faster now, with an ugly burr added to the whisper of its blades.

Then it didn't seem to matter any more, nothing seemed to matter except the cold spreading through his body, and the fact that the stars were fading away.

In a few moments that didn't matter either.

Thirteen

DOVE OF PREY

Everybody was talking and nobody was communicating. Maybe that wouldn't bother a Brazilian, but it was driving Captain Eric Burgess crazy. Worse: he was doing it himself, and for his life. He watched his instruments and kept his mouth shut; but inside, he seethed.

The tradition of the United States space effort had always been: *communication is life*. Ground base had to know *everything*; when something went wrong they could tell you what to try next; at worst they could tell the next man how you died. Silence violated Burgess' earliest training . . . but his life had been going gradually screwy ever since the government leased his contract to Brazil Techimetal-Electromotores.

He was forty-eight years old, a barrel of a man who fought constantly to keep his weight within regulated limits. This had little to do with laziness on his part. On the contrary, Burgess found his problem to be an expansiveness, a hunger for experiences and the exotic that sometimes exceeded his ability to safely assimilate them.

He had abandoned a sour marriage and an unspectacular career with NASA, when the Brazilian Air Force offered him a way out. Retirement would have driven him crazy.

But being kept on a leash in Sao Luis wasn't much better.

For a port city, Sao Luis was remarkably free from features of interest. It squatted nearly on the equator. His air conditioner would render the air barely thin enough to breathe. But he put up with the heat and the sopping clothes and the mosquitoes because he was paid to be close to the space facility, where once a month he rode the Shuttle *Brasilia* into orbit. Sometimes he and Ricardo Diaz, his copilot, would place satellites, or ferry up a pressurized "can" for zero-gravity industrial experiments. Once the "can" had been filled with Brazilian officials. It was a mess afterward; half of them had been sick.

He found he could talk to the officers of the Brazilian Air Force. Because many of them had once been pilots, they shared an empathy difficult with the politicians, and nearly impossible with the businessmen.

But in the two and a half years he had flown for Brazil, never had an assignment troubled him like this one.

Forty-eight hours ago he had been placed on alert, driven from his apartment in Sao Luis to the National Aerospace facility some thirty miles north. *Willy Ley*, the new Shuttle, had flown in piggy-back on a 747 just six weeks ago. It had had one shake-down run, and was supposed to be ready for the regular flight schedule. But there was nothing "regular" about the scene that greeted Burgess on his return to National Aerospace.

Two Shuttles were mounted atop their twin launch pads, bellies nestled to external tanks and solid rocket boosters. Brazil Techimetal-Electromotores' engineering consultant was with Colonel Olivera when Burgess reported for assignment. Burgess had met Lucio Giorgi before, and had not disliked the man: he carried his age with an old-world courtliness which Burgess admired. But that day the man seemed frozen; he spoke without communicating, without body language. Odd, in a Brazilian.

Colonel Olivera was heavier than Burgess, without the muscle to carry it well. He extended a sweaty palm and motioned to one of the office chairs.

"Captain Burgess," he said in his grueling Brazilian accent. "We wish to conduct a test of our emergency launch preparations."

"Fine. Is Diaz in yet?" His mind was

immediately immersed in *Brasilia*'s checkout procedures. "I expect you'll want us to get started immediately." The mugginess of the past few days in Sao Luis fell away like a cloak. This was more like it! "Are we having a dual launch? If we're doing that I'd like to get together with the captain of *Willy Ley*—"

Something in the air changed the instant he said that. It was as if Olivera and Giorgi had been waiting for him to ask that question, and were ready to explain something they didn't expect him to understand.

Olivera, his small black eyes watering slightly, looked back at Giorgi, who raised a single thin finger. The older man spoke, with the tone of a teacher lecturing an unfavored student. "*Brasilia* and *Willy Ley* will be performing separate functions during this exercise, and we feel it would be counterproductive to bring you together at this time."

"You're wondering if I can respond spontaneously? Wouldn't it be easier to test that in a simulator? This has got to be awfully expensive for a test."

"We consider the expense a worthwhile investment, Captain." There was dismissal in Giorgi's voice. Burgess didn't like it, but he took it.

The countdown began thirty-six hours later ... prematurely. A rescue mission. A Shuttle belonging to Falling Angel, the American industrial facility in lunar orbit, was in trouble. Burgess watched the UMAF's flat-faced zombie read her announcement, and could barely believe what he had heard.

When Olivera announced the rescue attempt, Burgess' first reaction was a fierce joy. The joy had faded to puzzlement at the last-minute addition of a BTE "mission specialist" to the crew. The new man was supposed to be a psychologist of some kind, there to report on stress reactions. That was thin stuff. Burgess tried to swallow it . . .

It wasn't until they had actually lifted through the light cloud cover, dropped the boosters at fifty kilometers and the external tank at a hundred and twenty, and were falling upward to meet *Anansi*, that the doubts really solidified.

It *had* to be coincidence that two Shuttles were ready to go when *Anansi* was attacked. After all, what could anyone possibly gain by such an attack? Only madmen . . .

His instructions were to take the crew of *Anansi* aboard, and take them down to safety. Then why was *Willy Ley* here? Their "mission specialist," Correro, had spoken with *Ley* several times, in Brazilian. But surely any spacecraft pilot would speak English?

There were too many separate things to bother him. The suspicion and hostility that showed through Captain De Camp's voice (and she wasn't saying anything either!), the ominous silence from *Willy Ley*, and perhaps more than anything else, the command to take orders from Correro—

Lost in his speculations, Burgess jumped when Ricardo Diaz pushed a foil-lined pouch of hot coffee into his hand. Diaz said, "It looks like we're going to have to wait, Eric."

Burgess nodded. Out of the corner of his eye he watched Correro. He and Diaz might have been brothers. Both were slender and strong, both tall, and their skin matched for tone. But Diaz was bright and cheerful, with razor-edged reflexes and an invaluable knack for second-guessing Burgess' needs.

Correro's eyes were the only part of his face that moved. He wore his headset consistently, listening to secret orders from Ground Control, murmuring back in Brazilian. Correro had watched with great interest as Thomas De Camp glided across space to the cargo pod.

"What's in there?" Burgess asked. "Just what were the terrorists after?"

Correro glared at him, spoke rapidly into his headset, pausing to listen to the reply. "It is a cable," he said finally. "Extremely valuable."

Cable? Dr. Dexter Stonecypher, Falling Angel's celebrated metallurgist, had been aboard. Hadn't he been working on some kind of super-cable? Burgess stirred around in his mind, looking for answers.

Salvage. Omigod. *That* was what the second ship was for, to take charge of the cable after the crew of *Anansi* went down. But all indications said that the "rescue" mission had been ready for days. And that meant—

He had to be wrong. But the doubt and suspicion continued to grow . . . and the fear.

"They're descending," Diaz said quietly. "I don't see how they can expect to do it. They lost too much fuel."

"I know . . . just stupid pride, I guess. Diaz, we'd better stay with them. They'll sure as hell need help."

Correro watched as the adjustment firing was made, then rose and clumsily made his way downstairs.

Diaz waited for the man's head to disappear down the stairwell, then nudged Burgess. "Something's wrong, Eric."

"You smell it too?"

The younger man shook his head vigorously. "I *heard* it. He is talking about guns. Some of what he said was in code, you know? Code words, but I heard 'guns.'"

"What do you make of it?" Burgess kept his voice down, and one eye on the stairwell.

"I think that someone has decided to guarantee their profits on this rescue mission. *Ley* is supposed to take the cargo if *Anansi* doesn't abandon it."

"But that's crazy—" There was a scuffing sound on the stairs. "—check your scope. The cable package *is* rising."

"What?" Correro propelled himself up the ladder and into the cabin, too quickly. He nearly cannoned into the seats, managing to check himself at the last second with a desperate grip on the chair back. Burgess concealed his contempt while Correro studied the screen. "Are you sure? They may have placed one of their limping motors on the cable pod."

"Limpet," Burgess said flatly. "Whatever it is, you'd better have *Ley* correct for it."

Correro barked into his microphone. They had no visual contact with the pod, but radar showed that it had risen above *Willy Ley*, and was continuing to gain altitude at about seven meters per second. The same rate, Burgess noted with interest, that *Anansi* was dropping, at least according to the computer. Burgess watched the other Shuttle rise past him . . . but his computer told him that *Brasilia*'s own orbit was contracting, that *Brasilia* was sinking.

A quick burst of attitude jets brought *Brasilia* and *Anansi* even again. A few minutes later he had to do it again. And the cable pod continued to rise . . .

Burgess scowled. "I don't understand what's happening here, Correro. *Anansi*'s rocket pods look like shredded lettuce! Where are they getting the thrust?"

"Are you so inferior a pilot, Burgess? I want you to stay with *Anansi*, do you hear me? Or can't you Americans take orders?"

"I'll do my best. I'm telling you, though, this is costing us fuel."

"And them, they must be using fuel too!"

Intuition spoke for Burgess. "I wonder. I don't know how they're—"

"I don't care!" Correro was screaming now. "I have my orders and you have yours!"

They stared at each other for long seconds, during which Burgess decided that he liked Correro less than any Brazilian he'd yet encountered. "All right, you're calling the shots. But I'll bet your friends in *Willy Ley* aren't doing much better."

They corrected three more times, and each time ended up dropping past *Anansi*, having to waste more fuel to come even again. Burgess had the distinct feeling that the unseen Captain De Camp was laughing at him, and was within a whisper of understanding why when his headphones broke into his train of thought.

It was Colonel Olivera. The officer's bluff voice had sharpened almost to a whine, and Burgess had little trouble sympathizing. "Captain Burgess—our ground computers are telling us very strange things. The *Anansi* is traveling too slowly to maintain its orbit."

"I can verify that. There doesn't seem to be any way for us to stay matched with them." He tuned his ears sharply now, waiting for the response to his next question. "I tell you what —why don't we just forget it? It's pretty clear that *Anansi* doesn't want to be rescued."

There was a blurred silence on the other end, marred by static. When Olivera came back on the line there was a new, ugly sound in his voice. "Captain Burgess. I want you to understand something. You will either complete your mission, or be arrested on landing."

"Say again. Arrested for what crime?"

"For refusal to follow the orders of your superiors. The contract which you signed with Brazil makes you an auxilliary member of our Air Force, subject to all rules and regulations of other military personnel."

"This isn't a military operation." Diaz was watching him with a kind of horrified fascination. "My contract was sublet to a civilian agency, which is apparently attempting a civilian salvage operation."

"Do not quibble with me, Captain Burgess. There is entirely too much at stake. You will follow our orders, or upon landing you will be turned over to a military court."

And shot. Burgess couldn't help filling in the rest of the threat. It was such absurd melodrama that he almost laughed.

And he almost, but not quite, asked: *And what if I don't land in Brazil? What if I ditch out somewhere that doesn't have an extradition treaty with Brazil?* Then he realized how close behind him Corerro was. Come to think of it, could Diaz be in on this too? Granted that the two of them, the Americano and the young Brazilian air force officer, had made the round of bars in Rio. Some of the better brothels, too. But what did that mean when you came right down to it? Just how big *was* this operation? Millions? Tens of millions at least. Olivera, he could be sure, had been well bribed. BTE had to be in this up to their wisdom teeth. It had cost one life already, and no *Americano* pilot was going to stand in the way now. That was what Correro was for.

"Talk to them, Burgess," Olivera said nastily. "Make them see that they must co-operate— or we will be forced to become un-pleasant."

There were questions, things that he wanted and needed to ask, but there was no-body on the line to answer, and he kept them to himself. *Talk to them?* His forehead was damp, but he didn't wipe it, didn't want to give Correro the satisfaction of seeing how shaken he was. What would he say? He knew now what Captain De Camp had suspected, knew why she didn't trust him. Hell, he was an accessory to murder. Within a few minutes it might get worse than that.

"All I wanted was a few more years," he said into the dead microphone.

"What was that, Eric?" Diaz's eyes were huge with questions. Burgess had questions too. *Can I trust Ricardo? How much does he know?* Diaz had his whole career ahead of him. This operation could guarantee the young Brazilian rank and fortune.

"I'm . . . sorry. I didn't realize I was talking out loud." Burgess looked out of his front window. *Brasilia* was almost directly above *Anansi*'s tail. The crippled ship was sliding away from him even as he watched. He could see directly into the cargo bay, could see that the bundles and packages intended for Oyama Construction had been lashed up against the sides of the ship, leaving a cleared floor space. He clucked to himself thoughtfully. It fit a pattern . . .

Anansi?

Years go, in a class on cultural anthropology, his teacher had discussed West African legends. Burgess fished through his mind and found Anansi, the archetypal spider who had climbed a silk line let down from heaven. Like the Japanese Susanoo and the Greek Haephestus and the Christian Lucifer, Anansi had worn out his welcome in Heaven. He had talked a dove into bringing him down again. Anansi was an unpleasant one; at the end of the flight he had eaten the bird. There was a moral there somewhere, but damned if Burgess could find it. He reached for the microphone.

"*Anansi*, this is Captain Burgess aboard *Brasilia*. Do you read me?" There was no reply, but he knew damned well that they heard him. What could they gain by communicating with him? "*Anansi* . . . I know that you're just trying to live up to your legend, but be a nice spider and talk to me, huh?" Still nothing. How far would he have to push it before De Camp knew that he knew? "Just consider me the dove of peace, come to take you safely home. Believe me, you could do a lot worse."

Behind him, Correro had stroked a slight bulge under his flight jacket. An unconscious movement, but a telling one. Is that where it is? Olivera would know that a regulation handgun would be no use in a pressurized vehicle. A miss could kill *everyone*. So what would it be? An air gun loaded with nerve darts?

"*Anansi*, please." He let his voice become a coo of sympathy, just a bit exaggerated. "You can't make it yourself, believe me. You need our help." *This time the dove is the predator.*

Still there was no answer.

Correro had made a decision. The "flight specialist" was tired of waiting. "All right, Burgess—" He deliberately smeared out the first syllable of the name in a long, nasty sound. "You've had your chance. The *Willy Ley* will take over from here. You are to exchange positions with the *Ley*, and guard the cable pod."

"Just what are you expecting *Ley* to do?" Burgess wasn't totally sure he wanted to hear, but part of him was fascinated, horrified but fascinated, by the drama unfolding around him. He didn't know what to do or whom to trust. Hasty action could get him killed. If, on the other hand, he kept his mouth shut and did as he was told, there might be enough in this for everyone. He hated himself for thinking that, but it didn't stop the image of golden coins from flashing into his mind.

"The *Willy Ley* will do what it must. You

will do as you are told, or Diaz will take control of the *Brasilia.*"

So. There it was. Burgess nodded silently and laid out his new course. The cable pod was eight kilometers from *Anansi* at that point, and still climbing.

Fourteen

THE KILLING PLACE

The air in the cabin had grown muggy. Without the solar panels on the ion drive, *Anansi*'s recycling equipment was lumbering along on batteries alone. The crew had killed all unnecessary power usage. Even if everything went exactly as they hoped, it would be a tight squeak.

But the mugginess had more to do with tension than with any quality of cabin atmosphere. Marion, Thomas, Janet, they sat lightly, stiffly, and their faces bore an intense, nearly identical *listening* look. They listened to their own bodies, to minute changes in the few pounds' weight of themselves against their chairs.

They were not watching their instruments. Given their present mode of transportation, the computers were quite useless.

Suddenly all three relaxed. "That's better," Marion said. "I thought we were hung up."

Thomas nodded; he'd felt it too. *Anansi* hung from the sky like a piano being lowered from a building, its nose tilted perhaps ten degrees upward. Moments ago Thomas's seat had surged upward, as if the cable were dragging. It was all right now . . . or was it? If the cable stopped unreeling, the tidal effect would still be pulling them gently downward—

"Damn it," Marion demanded, "are we moving or not?"

"Hard to tell . . . no, we're moving," Janet said. "About a kilometer every forty seconds. Call it thirty meters per second. At least we've still got the altimeter."

What they'd done was *working;* what more could he ask? But Thomas De Camp was a worrier. "Do we have any idea what the maximum rate of release is? We're already way above any speed Dexter could have anticipated. I picture little wheels getting hot inside the cable pod, with no way to cool them."

"We can hope Dexter used magnetic bearings," Marion said.

Janet was watching the radar screens. "We're certainly going to find out." She laughed. "*Brasilia*'s having her troubles. Every so often you see the motors flash, and she eases up to us and then drifts away again . . . wups. Something's going on. It looks . . .

Brasilia and *Willy Ley* seem to be headed for a summit meeting."

Both men craned to look past her. The two blips were drawing together on the screen. Thomas allowed himself the luxury of a moment of hope, gazed at the fragmented clouds still so far below them . . . but early optimism could get them killed.

"They're passing each other . . . they're changing places. *Tarzan* is swinging down to play."

"Oh, shit—I think you're right." Janet pushed away from the screen, turned her chair to face them. "Theories? What have they got on *Willy Ley* that could force us to stop?"

Marion held up a hand to tick off options. With small satisfaction, Thomas noted that the hand was not entirely steady. "Weapons, first of all."

"Not outside the ship; they'd burn off. Probably nothing big enough to blow us out of the sky, either. Even mounted in the cargo bay, we'd have seen it by now. If they'd known how much trouble we could give them, I think they would have just planted a mine inside the ship somewhere."

"Maybe they have, Janet." Thomas was talking from his pessimistic place, but he couldn't resist the temptation to answer his own implied question. "But we'd better assume they didn't. We've searched the cargo bay and found nothing. I've been all over the outside of the Shuttle, and there's nothing there. We *have* to assume that they thought they were going to do us enough damage with the first mine."

"All right, Thomas, tell me. Why do we *have* to assume that."

Thomas looked at Marion coldly. "They must know that we can't check every box in the cargo bay. Once they realize they can't catch us—*if* they can't, it's a bluff any moron would think of."

"Mmm. If we're wrong, we're dead anyway. Okay. It's a gamble . . . but this whole thing is a gamble." Marion's eyes were wide and almost boyish. He flicked at his hair in resignation; in the absence of gravity, it stayed flicked. "All right, then. The next possibility is men. Armed men, in mobile suits."

"Now *that's* a more likely possibility." Janet gripped Thomas' arm. "What do you think, Tommy? Can they do it? You've had more experience with the suits than either of us."

"The ships can't match orbits with us. We're under acceleration, however untraditional. *Willy Ley* might plot our course and drop some men off in an intersecting path . . . wait for us, then blast like hell with mobility units. Pretty tricky, but if they're good they might be able to do it." The inky negative thoughts roiled awhile, but once again he saw dark and bright sides both. "I'd bet they aren't much good. If they haven't figured out our play by *now* . . . Hey, Janet, what kind of game is Burgess playing? It sounded like he was trying to lay clues."

"I think he knows." She reached for his arm, and her grip was tight. "Why he didn't just come out and say what was on his mind, I don't know. Maybe . . ."

"Maybe what?"

"Oh, hell, I don't know. Maybe he's got qualms. But then what's he doing with the pirates in the *first* place? No, forget it."

"Forgotten." Marion tried to think of a third category. "Nope, it's guns or it's men with guns. The men might have recoilless rifles, maybe even a light rocket launcher. They'd have to be lucky to get aboard us—but not impossibly lucky. We'd better make plans. Shut the cargo bay doors?"

"We do that, they'll attack from outside. No. If they make it as far as *Anansi*, we want to take them on our terms."

"We'll need help," Thomas said. Somewhere in the back of Thomas' mind was the glimmer of an idea. "The emergency fire kits," he said, rising and heading toward the stairs. "How many CO_2 extinguishers do we have?"

When Marion joined Thomas on the lower deck, the ion drive tech already had the survival gear pulled out of the lockers, and had selected the flare kit and fire extinguishers for special consideration.

He was working on the first of two fire extinguishers with a screwdriver, his face tightened in concentration as he peeled the metal safety strip from around the bright red cylinder. "Just two, and lucky to get those," he said. "They'd never be used except on the ground. Fire in space, you just open the doors."

Marion watched a moment, then asked, "What can I do to help?"

De Camp flicked a glanced at him. "Ever work with explosives?"

"Only as a kid."

"That will have to do. I need the primers out of two of the flares. Be careful."

Marion took the latched plastic box that held *Anansi*'s emergency flares and anchored it next to Thomas at the work bench. Inside were two flare guns, and four flares nestled in styrofoam. A memory ticked . . . "Thomas, don't we have a .45 or something? A lot of the old emergency kits had them. In case you set down in hostile territory or something?" He peered at the back end of one of the flares and saw the shallow circular rise of the primer, set dead-center in the rear of the shell.

"I looked. Maybe there was one, long ago. I'd guess nobody thought it was important enough to replace. We'll just have to do the best we can." Thomas' strong stubby fingers were busy unscrewing the nozzle from the fire extinguisher. He looked up, vacantly. "How much time do we have?" He reached out and flicked on the intercom, rather than yelling up the ladder well. "Janet? Do you have *Ley* on your scope? Or a visual yet?"

The flared nozzle came free and he glared at the remainder of the extinguisher: safety ring, valve, and the thumb trigger that would send a steel needle through the metal foil sealing the cylinder.

"*Ley* is ahead of us and still about four kilometers up, Tommy."

"Good." He glanced at Marion, who had worked the flare free of its shell. "If we don't blow ourselves to hell, I should have our surprise ready in about twenty minutes." He clicked off the intercom and went back to his work: loosen a base screw, carefully twist the valve free . . .

"Yeah," Marion said absently sorting through Thomas' magnetic tool rack until he found needle-nosed pliers. "I did a little fooling around when I was a kid. Nothing really special . . . except once."

"Once?"

"Yeah." Marion had adjusted the swanneck lamp to peer directly over his shoulder, so that the light went right down into the shell. He inserted the pliers and groped carefully. "I was a preppy—Air Force preppy. Dad sent me to military school so I'd be officer material. Anyway, I made some enemies in high school." He had hold of something at the bottom of the shell, and twisted slowly. "Bruiser named Oscar. Oscar Irving. I wrote poetry at the time— terrible stuff, I did the world a great service by becoming an astronaut—ah!" He held the primer up to the light. It was an inch long, little thicker than a lead pencil.

Thomas smiled approval. "That's good. And quick, too. Get me another one and we're in business." He had almost finished stripping his first extinguisher, right down to the foil. He looked at the silvery cap and whistled softly. "Wish I knew a better way of doing this. . ." He took an electric etcher and carefully scored the top of the cap with a cross-marking. "Just want to weaken this a little." Marion was silent while Thomas made his delicate operation. He only realized that he had stopped breathing when the cylinder was pushed to the side and carefully moored in place. Thomas smiled weakly. "Anyway. What happened?"

"Mmm?"

"At your school." Thomas lifted the next extinguisher on end and scrutinized it.

"Oh, yeah. Well, I had a locked desk, and someone kept beaking into it. Brute force, he'd just yank the drawer open hard enough to break the lock. He'd steal the poems and post them on the bulletin board. It happened twice, and everybody knew who was doing it . . ." He went to work on the second shell. His expression was somewhere between concentration and reverie.

"I had access to the chem lab. I precipitated some nitrogen tri-iodide." He glanced over at

Thomas, saw the pursed smile surface and smooth over again. "Ah, you know of it. I didn't have any trouble getting iodine crystals and ammonia. I had some trouble getting hold of ether to wash it. Seems that two cadets had been dismissed the semester before for getting high on the stuff, and the professor kept it locked safely away. I had to go out and buy some."

"Simplicity is the mark of genius," Thomas said. "Go on."

"I made up about a quarter-ounce of the stuff, and painted it all over the inside of my desk. I took the bulb out of the ceiling light, left the room and proceeded to tell everybody I'd just written the best poem of my entire life, I was going to enter it in a state literary contest . . . I knew Oscar couldn't resist that. I made sure I was in the rec hall that night, visibly stuffing quarters in the video games, you know, anything to keep me out of the way—" Triumphantly he held up his second primer. "All right, what do we do with them?"

"Just hold on for now, and get me two extension cords, the kind that clip into the cargo bay light sockets."

"Got it."

Thomas had almost finished with the second extinguisher when the intercom came back on. "Tommy, *Willy Ley* is closing on us from behind. They've set up an intercept orbit. We'll be on them in about ten minutes. No way to maneuver. Are you ready down there?"

Thomas wiped at his forehead, trying to control his breathing. "Almost, Janet." The second extinguisher was naked except for the foil cap, and he carefully scored it. "Five minutes."

Aware that his movements were growing erratic and jerky, Thomas forced calm into his hands, searched through his cabinet for the putty. He took the first primer and friction-taped it to the tip of the electric etcher, then attached the taped bundle to the top of the fire extinguisher, molding it tight with putty.

When he had done the same with the second etcher and the second fire extinguisher, he looked at both of the jerry-rigged devices and shuddered. "Damn—if only we had more time . . ." Then shook his head and started for the suit rack, taking down his helmet. "Marion, plug the etchers into the cords, but *don't* plug the cords in."

The inside of Thomas' suit smelled of sweat and dried blood; there had been no time to clean it. He flexed his knee and sighed. "I'll have to fight in this stink. Are you finished?"

Marion held up the plugs. Each fire extinguisher was now attached to a thirty-foot length of extension cord.

"Good. Better suit up. And finish your story."

The copilot grinned. "You could finish it yourself. About nine thirty that night we hear a muffled explosion. Oscar comes screaming into the rec room, howling bloody murder. His hands and face are dead purple, and so is his shirt. You know nitrogen tri-iodine: it's perfectly safe when wet, but when it dries it'll go off if a fly lands on it, and it leaves that iodine stain all over everything. Oscar was the Purple Man for a couple of days. He had a wonderful time explaining to the Headmaster exactly how it all happened, and what he was doing in my desk. I never had any more trouble after that."

Thomas chuckled, and helped Marion into his suit. It smelled no better than Thomas'. "You're not too bad, Guiness."

"The worst part of it for poor Oscar was that he didn't even get one of my better poems. It went something like, 'Roses are red, violets are blue, orchids are purple and so are you—' "

Janet's voice, low and urgent, interrupted their laughter. "Tommy, Marion, listen to me. I've got my camera on *Willy Ley*. They've dropped off three EVA's. Mobility suits and what look like rifles, maybe light rocket launchers. We'll intersect their path in about four minutes."

Thomas and Marion sealed each other's helmets on, and gripped hands, hard. "Let's do this right," De Camp said soberly. "We'll only have one chance. Janet? Do you read me?"

"Clear, Tommy."

"Good, then cycle us through the airlock.

And one more thing: I want you to kill all
power in the cargo bay . . ."

* * *

The men who waited for *Anansi* were
known as Strike Leader, Wolf One and Wolf
Two. They were Brazilian mercenaries, and
had sold their services in South America and
Africa for the past eight years, fighting in full-
scale wars and minor skirmishes. One job had
been an assassination of a Bolivian priest who
had caused much trouble for the mining com-
panies, speaking out against the deplorable
working conditions which supposedly existed
in the camps. A bundle of high explosive
wired to the ignition of the priest's Jeep had
proved an effective rebuttal to his charges.

But there had never been *anything* like this.
Strike Leader knew that he should have re-
jected the commission out of hand. His team
wasn't even BTE's first choice, and he knew it.
Their fee would be sufficient for a comfortable retirement. He would have a name
again; he might even publish his memoirs ("As
told to . . .") But none of these would have
been reason enough.

He'd thought he could back out if the training went badly.

There had been two weeks of briefings that
resembled high school physics courses, interrupted by weightlessness training in water
tanks and in airplanes swooping through par-

abolic arcs. The team had lost Wolf Three: weightlessness sent him into screaming hysterics. *Wolf Three wasn't good enough.* It was too late then. Strike Leader had accepted the challenge.

The lure of deep space had entered his soul via American movies with subtitles: *2001* and *Star Trek* episodes and *Moonraker* and *Star Wars*; but Strike Leader didn't know that. He knew only what he felt: a fiery anticipation of war in space. One day it had to come. Strike Leader ached for the glory of being first.

He checked the positions of Wolves One and Two. They flanked him, twenty meters to either side, and he motioned them forward to form a rough triangle. He watched them floating on their way, backlit by the reddish flare of a rising sun: a vista of eerie beauty, a strangeness he'd known only via science fiction movies and television; a sensation he'd probably never experience again.

He could be losing himself in the glory about him when an enemy took his life; but there were other matters to distract him. He was loaded down like a donkey: the bulky inflated suit, the massive mobility unit, his weapon, the narrow-beam radio poking from his helmet like a single huge ear. Every motion was an effort, free fall or no. He forced his attention onto his oxygen level, the positioning of Wolves One and Two, the violent work to come.

He fingered his weapon, an automatic rifle

capable of firing thirty rounds of explosive ammunition per second. He felt confident that it would punch through five centimeters of fused alumino-silicate glass, leaving the captain and crew of *Anansi* splattered around the command module like so many squashed insects. All that preparation for a few minutes of real work. It was always that way, unless things went wrong.

He wagged himself from side to side with his mobility harness, giving it a last test. His suit-to-suit link came to life. "Strike Leader, this is Wolf Two. I have visual contact."

"*Willy Ley*, this is Strike Leader. What is your estimation of intercept time?"

The voice from *Willy Ley* was thin and nervous. Strike Leader did not much like the sound: a weak man on Transportation could ruin the most tightly-planned operation. "Approximately ninety seconds, Strike Leader."

He could see *Anansi* against an arc of Earth's horizon, a wedge shape that wouldn't have covered a postage stamp, but visibly growing. He and his men fell toward the enemy like a handful of flung pebbles. They should have had time to practice with the mobility units.

"Strike Leader, *Anansi* is still under acceleration. Her speed relative to you is now approximately fifteen kilometers per hour. Eighteen. Twenty—"

Anansi was almost the size of an envelope now, and as he watched she seemed to balloon in his sight, frighteningly fast.

"Wolf One!" he barked. "Move out!" He turned his mobility unit jets up to full, and hot gas hissed forward, past him. *Anansi's* approach slowed, slowed. Wolf Two, scrambling to get out of the path of the hurtling juggernaut, triggered his jets in the wrong direction, accelerating directly into it. There was a brief squeal of pain, followed by the shriek of a dying radio. Strike Leader caught a brief glimpse of a dark hunchback-shape tumbling helplessly away, limbs twitching spasmodically.

They should have had time to practice! But Strike Leader himself was above *Anansi's* cargo bay, firing attitude jets sideways, then dropping between the curved double doors even as the jets continued to slow him. He felt savage satisfaction. He would make *Anansi* suffer for this loss . . .

Where was Wolf One?

No sign, anywhere. He gritted his teeth, hissing out a long string of filthy words, transmuting his fear into smouldering anger. The silence, the total *alienness* of the surroundings had to be pushed far back, back into a corner, so that he could operate from the Killing Place.

He had found the Killing Place in the African desert, he had found it in the jungles of Brazil and the backroads of Bolivia. It was a place where the gentle emotions swirled out beyond the periphery of consciousness, and the harsh feelings—fear, anger, lust—combined to burn a hole in his mind, making a concentrated furnace, a white-hot place where nothing existed except total commitment. Once he found the Killing Place he was set, ready for whatever came.

But his own breath echoed in his ears, and it sounded frightened, even to him.

He peered into the bay, hampered by the mobility pack. He itched to take it off, but didn't dare to, quite yet. Strike Leader shone a light down into the bay. Its dull white circle glanced off stacks of bundles lashed to the walls. These were things his employers wanted. Otherwise he would have fired bursts in all directions, as a simple precaution. The Shuttles didn't carry much in the way of weaponry, but he had improvised death himself often enough to know to take no chances.

There were entirely too many shadows, too much darkness. Which way was the airlock? If they didn't let him through he had the explosive to blow the door clean off its hinges. Find out what the crew would do with a lungful of vacuum. In fact, with his backup men gone, perhaps he should do that, and to hell with their chance to surrender. How *would* human beings die in vacuum?

His light caught a glimmer of something on the floor. A trap? He stayed motionless while he studied it. Two rows of metal disks . . . and a glint in the air, right in front of him, like a line of spiderweb where sunlight caught it.

A thread. Anchored to the floor and stretching up into the blackness beyond. Could this . . . *this* . . be the cable that his employers were after? He almost laughed, and the sudden absurdity wiped away much of his tension, and he found himself calm once again. Now then, to business.

He headed for the airlock door. There was weight here, minute weight, different from Earth and different from what he had learned of free fall. Therefore he walked with care, aware that a trained enemy might have the advantage.

An unfamiliar voice spoke over his suit's speaker, saying in English: "Power!"

In the back of the cargo bay, two lights went on. To either side of him there were silent explosions, and he automatically dropped to the ground, or tried to. The reflexive maneuver left him hugging his knees and tumbling in mid-vacuum. Even in mid-tumble he tried to orient, to bring his weapon to bear as the floor spun past his line of sight. But his vision was clouded, filled with white mist that belched from both sides at once, and he fired blind. *Damn*! Where were they?

He saw a flash of light and twisted clumsily, stifling a scream as something punched through the fog at him, streaking past his chest at ferocious speed.

The second flash took Strike Leader full in the side before he ever saw it. He was smash-

ed back into a wall of cases, dazed, surprised
to be alive. Then he heard the sucking whistle,
looked down at the fluttering burn hole in his
suit, and knew that he wasn't.

The urge for self-preservation warred with
a need to deal death. Strike Leader tried to
compromise: he covered the hole with one
arm, while the assault rifle chattered in his
other hand. Cargo crates erupted in showers
of metal and plastic. The cloud of carbon dioxide crystals fragmented, boiling up out of the
open hatch until the entire bay was frosted
with thinning wisps of vapor.

One burst, before Strike Leader realized he
was still leaking. His ears spewed air; they
felt like ice picks had been jabbed into them.
Now he used both arms to block the burn-
hole, too late. His body tried to expand like a
balloon: irresistable pressure in belly and
guts and lungs. His sphincters wouldn't hold
the agonized fart, the explosion of foamy
vomit across his faceplate; but he did try to
hold his breath. His instructors had said that
was a mistake. He remembered that when he
felt his lungs tearing apart.

He thrashed, bouncing off the floor and upward. He tried to sip air from his hissing
recycler, but it was still thinner than what
was in his lungs. His arms were still trying to
block the burn hole, to hold near-vacuum confined in his suit. Blind, deaf, nearly senseless,
he felt himself expanding without limit. He
had faced death in reality and in fearful

dreams, but never like this, with his scream silenced and his guts still trying to empty him further.

The humiliation was too much to bear. The first battle in space, and his unarmed victims had killed him. Thank God nobody knew his name.

Fifteen

PENDULUM

Marion stepped out from between two stacks of cargo crates. He was shaking badly. Right next to his hiding place, Strike Leader had made a direct hit, shattering a sack of viscous fluid. It formed itself into rough globules, floating through the bay like dark amber soap bubbles. One floated toward his faceplate, boiling sluggishly, expanding. He brushed it away with the tip of his flare gun, hoping that it wasn't any kind of corrosive.

"Thomas? Are you all right?" At the opposite wall, there was movement as one of the carefully wrapped bundles was pushed aside. The little ion tech looked up at the drifting body of Strike Leader.

There was a note of savage satisfaction in Thomas' voice. "We got him. I can't believe it.

We actually *got* him!"

"Tommy! Is everything through down there? What happened?"

"Only one came down, Janet. Did you see what happened to the other two?"

"One rammed us. Probably regretted it. I can't find the third. Any damage? *Are either of you hurt?*"

Thomas looked Marion over, then scanned the cargo bay. The air was filled with vapor and dust and speckles of blasted metal. Of perhaps three hundred stacked and labeled boxes, about twenty had been damaged.

Thomas probed around in one of the boxes, pulled out a handful of shattered nylon gears. "It's pretty bad down here, but it could be a lot worse. I'm not hurt, Marion's not hurt. We've lost some cargo. But it looks like the boxes absorbed the bullets . . . maybe saved us a broached hull."

"If that's all, that's good news. *Ley* is just sitting there. They've been eating up a lot of fuel, and about now they must be making some tough decisions."

Marion laughed. "I'd like to be in on the vote. What do we do now?"

"We've lost about eighty miles altitude—" Janet's voice changed, lowering almost to a growl. "Well, well—*Willy Ley* seems to be dropping out of the game. At least they're dropping off my scope. Good, that leaves us with *Brasilia*. I wouldn't think they're as dangerous, given they were supposed to take us down to Earth."

"Still hovering around the cable pod?"

"Right, and burning fuel every time they want to get close."

"What have they got in mind? They've got seven hours to do something," Thomas said. "Let's be careful. I want to do any clean-up we can, and then get back out of this suit."

"Good enough. See you when you're through."

"Anansi?" Fleming's voice carried concern, fear and anger across a quarter million miles of emptiness, pulling Janet out of a half-doze, nudging her back toward useful thought.

"Read you, Angel. Things are getting a little wiry. Lost track for a second. I won't let it happen again." *Can't sleep!* She wiped her forehead, found it already dry.

She watched the sweeping arc on the radar screen delineate two tiny blips. *"Brasilia* is way out of camera range, almost off the scope. *Willy Ley* is closer, but doesn't seem to want to play any more."

It was two and a half seconds—the light-speed gap—before Falling Angel's elder statesman said, "I don't blame them. Now, we've received verification that *Brasilia* and *Ley* were both under lease to BTE. I should have trusted Kelly's feelings."

"Sir?"

"Never mind. What *is* important is that it's all out in the open, now that you've broken

radio silence. We will communicate with
Oyama Construction on this, and that will get
things moving on Earth." There was a
dampening sorrow to his voice. "You know,
nobody would have dared try such a thing
while we were part of NASA. The whole world
knows how helpless we are. Maybe I . . ."

Janet's fingernails grated on the metal of
the control display. She could finish the
thought for him: *Maybe I shouldn't have
bucked the system. Too late. Now we're clay
pigeons for anyone who wants what we've
got . . .*

"No, Doctor," she snapped. "We've done
what we had to do. We have to fight and we
have to win, or they'll roll all over us next
time!"

"Yes. Sorry." Fleming had taken savage
shocks in the last few hours: Dexter Stonecypher's death, the crippling of *Anansi*, the
bandit spacecraft, all had taken their toll. His
voice had thinned until it seemed an old
man's. "You've described your mode of
descent, and our computers back you. It can
be done. But you'll need emergency landing
facilities: crash nets, ambulance, fire
trucks—"

"We can still make Okinawa. I see no
reason to change plans."

"Fine, but we'll set up your alternate sites. I
want no mistakes. You people are coming
back, dammit. I'm not losing any more of
you."

Janet felt her lips curling into a smile, and forgot her fatigue. "You won't. Goodby, Doctor."

"Hold the fort." And he was gone.

A light blinked on the board: airlock in use. Thomas and Marion were back. She heard them talking on the lower level, garbled words that seemed a mixture of serious discussion and morbid humor.

Janet was starting to realize how tired she was. How long had it been since she had slept? Twenty hours? Something like that. But in spite of the danger, and the almost intolerable stress, she felt absurdly happy that the three of them were working so well together. Tommy seemed more alive and spontaneous than he had in months, and Marion . . . Well, Marion seemed very good at following directions, but a little weak on establishing them.

She smiled sourly. A hell of a time to be making comparisons between ex-lover and soon-to-be-ex husband.

Or is it? After all, I put Marion aboard. Husband and lover and me, all cozy in a tiny Shuttle cabin, millions of miles from any distraction . . . theoretically. What would a good shrink make of that?

Janet watched her hands shake, felt her fingers curling as if caressing a cigarette. *Funny . . . haven't wanted tobacco in years . . .*

Thomas was first up the ladder, and he nodded to her. "What do you think? Did we get all three of them?"

"We may never know. I can't find that third bandit. If he's falling free he'll be a hundred miles down by now. Maybe he got back to *Willy Ley*. Anyway, all we have to worry about is *Brasilia*."

Marion eased into his seat, and Janet couldn't help but appreciate the grace with which he moved. Free fall was paradise for the lazy, but it was Marion's element too. She checked the air temperature, expecting to find that it had risen a few degrees, then realized that it was just her. *My God, am I turned on? That's absurd!*

"How much more cable is there?" Thomas' hand on her arm made her start: his fingers were hot.

"Ahh . . ." Come *on*. Focus your mind, woman! "We've unreeled about a hundred and ten kilometers already. If nothing else goes wrong, we'll be in the atmosphere in six hours. Cut the cable and fly in. Japan in seven hours."

"Good. I think I've had about all of this I want." Thomas rubbed at his eyes. "I feel like my glands have been pumping me full of Greek fire. Somewhere down there I must be tired unto death, but it's a little hard to find, you know?"

Marion looked at Thomas curiously. The man's face was full of shallow creases that hadn't been there a day ago, and a haunted look had deepened his eye sockets. He could have been five years older. When he moved, there was a tight-skinned caution about him, as if he thought his shell might burst.

"I tell you what," Marion said impulsively. "When we get to Tokyo, I want to buy the three of us the biggest steaks we've had in years. Not that freeze-dried muck at *Falling Angel*, but three fearsome slabs of Kobi beef." He could *taste* it: almost a true hallucination. "Beer-fattened. Dripping with sizzling juice. Garnished with slivered, quick-fried vegetables."

"Wokked?"

"Thomas, I don't care if they *ever* got enough exercise as long as they're fresh—"

Thomas guffawed and swung at him, and the three laughed together, the laugh fading to quiet as they really looked at each other for the first time. Janet clucked sadly. "We're quite a trio, aren't we? Here we are, three intelligent, creative people who can start from nothing and whip a billion-dollar conglomerate. And we can't even sort our own lives."

Thomas' smile winked off a bit, then flashed back, crooked now. "I'm better with things than people, Janet. I don't have anyone to blame but me, really." He reached out to squeeze Marion's arm. "Can't blame you, either. Janet is . . . a lot of lady. I'd probably do pretty much what you did."

"Oh, that's ridiculous," Marion said peevishly. "You'd never be able to deal with a *sometime* woman. You'd want to propose, just like you did the first time."

Thomas opened his mouth, and Janet shushed him in protest. "Wait a minute, what is this, group therapy at 200,000 feet?"

"Why not?" Marion wondered. "Six hours to go, dangling like an ambitious spider. Psychoanalysis can be fun."

Janet seemed to struggle for words. "Oh, what the hell. Tommy, Marion, I owe you both an apology. I think maybe I wanted the two of you here with me."

"Why?"

"Because I hate to fail, dammit, and I failed with you, Tommy. I couldn't ever compete with your machines. Maybe I thought, if you saw me interacting with Marion, if you could really *see* that it was over, *feel* that it was over . . ." By the dull light in the cockpit she looked haggard, the brilliant gold of her hair washed out into a pale straw.

Marion gave a low whistle. "I guess I could have figured something. You pressured me hard. Hum. I was supposed to be on exhibit? And Dexter for a referee, maybe?"

The floor surged up against Thomas' Velcro slippers, and his hand snaked out for the back of the control chair before he realised what it meant. "Oh, shit, it was just getting interesting."

They felt it too. The floor pressing up against their feet, then easing. Marion opened his mouth, and the floor surged again.

"It's sticking and releasing and sticking. What the—" The pressure eased to a tenth gravity; surged; eased away. Marion said, "Someone's on the cable pod. Trying to jam the cable, or cut it."

The floor surged again; held for several seconds. They waited it out. It eased off, slowly.

Thomas said, "I'd guess they don't have the tools. We're talking *Brasilia*, the goddam treacherous dove that was going to take us down from Heaven. Any obvious weapons, any special tools for hijackers, wouldn't they be aboard *Willy Ley*, where we couldn't notice them? Cutting into the cable pod would be a tremendous job. Maybe a torch would cut the cable, but they won't do that either, because they want it. So . . . you're right. They're trying to jam it."

"Dammit, no! They *can't get aboard* the cable pod. They can't match orbits," Janet protested. "Don't you see, the cable pod isn't *in* an orbit, it's hanging from the sky like another spider, under tidal gravity. If—" The floor surged.

Thomas kept talking. "One bandit got aboard *us*. I think they put someone aboard the cable pod. Now, what could he use to jam the cable?"

"With that line running out at . . . Janet, you said forty meters per second? It'd cut through steel, easy."

"Something harder than steel, then. Synthetic diamond or sapphire: the faceplate from a pressure suit. And it *is* cutting through, cutting notches in the wedge, can't you feel it? The poor bastard has to keep pulling the wedge out and jamming it in again different." Ghost of a smile on Thomas' face.

"Not any more," Janet said. "Check the altimeter. We've stopped."

Into the silence Marion asked, "How far down are we, Janet?"

"A hundred and sixty kilometers below our original orbit. Three hundred and twenty from the cable pod. That's it. *Brasilia's* jammed the cable. We're stuck."

Earth's horizon rose into view past Janet's head; paused, then began to set. The configuration was swinging in a vast arc, a pendulum isolated in space, weighted at each end, swinging from its center.

"Well," Marion said slowly. "What next?"

Nobody answered. "Cut the cable," Marion suggested. "Hope we're low enough to drop into the atmosphere. Give the bandit on the cable pod a hell of a shock. He'll rise so high that *Brasilia* won't be able to rescue him and still get down ... no?" Because Thomas was shaking his head.

"We don't have to hope," he said. "We can do the math, but I already know the answer. We're not low enough or slow enough."

Janet asked, "Tommy ... how much range do we have on the mobility units?"

He barked laughter. "Nothing like enough.

I'd never make it up."

Beneath them, Earth was a hazy blue sheet with a subtly curved horizon. "Close enough to taste . . ." Janet bit her lip painfully hard, then slammed her fist down on her knee. "No! We can't be beaten now. Tommy, isn't there something? Some way to get up to that pod?"

"I'm stale. I'm out of ideas, Janet. I'm sorry." He looked miserable, hollow, as if he were collapsing in on himself.

"Not so fast," Marion said. "We've got some time. *Brasilia* can't *do* anything. They probably wouldn't cut the cable even if they could. They may have to wait for turn-around time on *Willy Ley*, have it bring up special tools . . . a missile, maybe. Blow us away and collect the cable. But we've got *hours*." He was trying to project hope in his voice and his thinnish face, but Janet knew it was mostly bluff.

Thomas' eyes were focussed on some distant point, as if something Marion had said had stuck in his mind rather than just pouring through the mesh. He folded his hands and set his chin on laced fingers . . . feeling their eyes, hearing their silence as they let him think . . . Presently he asked, "Exactly what are we carrying in all those crates? It's all equipment for handling the cable. Let's get an inventory."

Janet brought the list up from the main computer, displayed it on the center screen. "Any idea what you're looking for? No? Cable

collars, epoxy . . ." Her eyes scanned the list.
" . . . lubricant, motorized cutters . . . pulleys,
staples, tackle . . ."

Thomas cut in. "Tackle? Give me the specs.
Tackle as in block and tackle?"

Janet tickled the computer's memory. "As
in fishing tackle, I'd say." The image looked
like a cross between a geared fishing tackle
and a C-clamp.

"No. It's for the construction workers. They
can rappel down or climb along the cable with
it." His gaze was reflective.

"Tommy!" Janet realized what her husband
was thinking, and objected instantly. "You
can't pull yourself along three hundred kilometers of cable! That gripper isn't even
motorized."

"Doesn't need to be. The gear ratio is enormous; look at it! Just like the cutters—"

"No. I don't like it, we'll have to find
another way. They'll see you coming!"

"Not from *Brasilia* they won't. I'll be too
small, and they won't be anywhere near the
cable pod most of the time. Whoever they've
got on the cable won't have radar. I'll fall on
him like a bomb."

Marion asked, "Why do you keep saying—"

"No. Me. Janet needs you for the landing."

"DAMN IT, TOMMY!" She was screaming
before she realized it, caught herself clumsily.
"You're not expendable. Not at all. I'd swear
that you keep manipulating things so that you
have to take all the risks, except . . . except

that that's not quite you, either."

Marion grunted aloud. "Maybe it is. Janet, I think that you had better tell this man that I'm the one with the muscles. It'll take maximum muscle, Thomas."

"No. It's almost zero gee, and when I get past the midpoint I can *slide* down. Hey, do you think I *want* to play hero? I know where my priorities are, that's all."

Marion stared at him. "I bet you do. I wouldn't blame you for wanting a white hat. Janet, if you know where your own priorities are, tell this man that you love him."

Janet's mouth was numbly open as she tried to see through Thomas' mask to the workings within.

"Janet, will you *tell him?* Your husband is about to go and commit suicide to get your approval—"

"Oh, cut it out!" Thomas snapped, then fell silent.

"Tommy? Tommy, look at me."

He wouldn't; he glared at the floor as if his life depended on it.

"See?" Marion started up from his chair. "This time, *I* go."

"Wait just a minute, Marion." Thomas looked up. "Maybe my motivations are mixed up, but it'll still take two pilots to land this ... bullet-riddled, bomb-blasted, crippled wreck, assuming it's possible at all. No amount of macho theatrics can change that. If either of you has any real reasons why I should be here instead of up there, I'd be glad to hear them."

"Tommy," Janet said softly, "I *love* you."

He smiled, and she knew she had said the right thing . . . but O God, the timing! Because Thomas said, "I guess that's as good a reason as any to go, isn't it?"

"You'll die. You can't carry enough air. The survival hut on *Gabriel* was blown to shreds. What are you going to *breathe?*"

"Marion breathes too. Listen. We're hanging here like a *piñata* waiting for the Brasilians to take pot-shots at us. We have to take the initiative, and unless I get a better suggestion, this is it." He looked at the co-pilot, whose eyes were squeezed shut. "Marion? Anything? . . . No, I thought not. I'd better get going."

Janet got up. "Marion, take charge here. I want to . . . help Tommy get suited up."

"Sure."

Thomas was already thinking through the fastest way to find the tackle—so many damaged crates!—when he heard Janet lifting the ceiling grid into place behind her. She shook her head, and her hair fluffed out in a pale halo, framing a face that was drawn, but softened with concern. She pushed herself down from the ladder, with practiced ease guiding herself over to him.

Her voice was almost timid. "Have you . . . have you replaced the recycler element? You'll want as much time as possible before

. . . damn." She stopped herself in mid-sentence. His suit still hung out on the rack, not yet cleaned or deodorized, and she ran her hands over it, a dull, wordless ache emptying her chest.

Her husband checked over his equipment, carefully sorting out the necessities for his last few hours of life. She could almost see him checking off items on his mental file-cards. He had withdrawn far into that quiet, lonely place where no one ever trespassed.

"Tommy . . . ?" She reached out to grasp his shoulder. The muscle under his shirt tensed reflexively, and he ignored her, until she dug her fingers into his skin painfully hard. *Look at me.*

When he turned his eyes were a little too bright, and she realized, thankfully, that the man within him was very much alive, and that only his self-control kept the sheen of tears from encapsuling his eyes. "I guess this is it, Janet." He was having trouble meeting her gaze; his speech was a little thick. "I just want you to know . . . how much . . . I appreciate you."

"Oh, Tommy, can't you say it?" Her voice was low and husky, and she was very near him now, her lips a breath away, her arms entwining his shoulders like thick warm vines. "Can't you?" He turned his face away, but his body betrayed him, arcing forward to press against her.

His mouth worked, but nothing came out.

Janet ran her fingers gently through his hair and said, "Shhh . . ." and something inside Thomas De Camp broke. Suddenly he was holding her, and their lips were melting together, and their hands were ripping Velcro strips apart. Janet gasped, shocked at the intensity with which they gripped each other, as if they were two seventeen-year-old virgins intoxicated with first lust.

Then her legs were around him at the hips, and she had kicked off her shoes. She gripped the netting with her fingers and toes, forcing his back into it as they tried desperately to say all of the things that had never been said, knowing that it was too little, too late.

It was too volcanic to last more than a matter of minutes. Seconds, really, but time was an artificial construct, far from her reality, when Janet opened her eyes and looked at her husband.

He laughed uncertainly, and licked at a moist patch on her neck. "Well . . . I'll have to volunteer for suicide duty more often."

She wanted to hit him, hurt him, shut him up, anything to keep those last few moments from slipping away too quickly, but his dark joke had worked, made her laugh against her will. And the mood broke, there was nothing left to do but complete the work that had to be done.

So they cleaned the inside of the pressure suit in savage haste, and plugged in an unused breathing-air system, and then she helped him into it and made his last-minute checks for him. She kissed him a last time, and sealed his helmet into place . . . sealed him into his tiny death-chamber, and watched him cycle through the airlock, watched the light blink to red.

Then she straightened her clothes, and wiped her face with a pre-moistened, disposable towelette. And with a final glance at the unblinking red light, she climbed back up to the control level, to see through the rest of her role.

Sixteen

MANEUVERING

The cable pod was coming into sight through *Brasilia*'s windows. A bright dot, above and behind the Shuttle, catching up fast. Burgess watched his distance decreasing in the radar scan, took a guess, and fired a burst from the forward jets. "This is driving me nuts," he said.

"I do not expect you to moor to the pod." Correra spoke with what he probably thought of as commendable patience. "I accept that that is impossible, since Ground Control confirms your claim. Only come close. Observe, then call Diaz, learn his situation."

A good ground team might have worked out a computer program for the cable pod's peculiar acceleration, in weeks or months. Never in hours. Burgess was flying without

computers for the first time since flight
school. It bothered him as much as Correra
did.

He tuned the radio. "Ricardo?"

"Captain Burgess! Is that you?"

"Who else?"

Ragged breathing. "I am very much alone
here. How long has it been, two hours?
More?"

"I thought I'd done pretty well. I'm in an
elliptical orbit with an apogee that puts me
right next to you every two hours. I could pick
you up now if I had to," he said, ignoring Correro's violent headshake. "What's your situation?"

The exhaustion showed in Diaz's voice. "The
cable is not moving. I can barely see it, but I
tied a strip of cloth to it. The cable was cutting
grooves in the cutter blade I've been using for
a wedge. I have had to shift it and pound it
back in, over and over. My arms are ready to
drop off. No problems with the suit. In a few
minutes I should change tanks. That will give
me another four hours of oxygen. Is there any
reason for me to stay here?"

Now the cable pod looked like a plume of
desert rock, sculpted by wind and flood, floating against the night in clear defiance of
common sense. At the base of the wide blunt
fins a light glimmered in shadow: Diaz, watching to see that the cable didn't pop his wedge.

Correra was shaking his head again. Burgess simply handed him the microphone. Cor-

rera returned his look of contempt while he spoke into it. "You will remain on duty until our next pass. Then return."

He handed the mike back, and Burgess turned if off before he spoke. "I don't see the point in this. We've stopped the cable. *Anansi* can't go down and can't go up. We're just waiting for *Willy Ley* to come back."

"Three hours ago it was impossible for them to alter their orbit. Now it is impossible for them to counterattack. Tchaa! How long must we wait for *Willy Ley?*"

Burgess mulled the problem. Landing and safety inspection for the Shuttle would be quick, only about an hour. Maintenance. Loading in the new payload: equipment to convert the cable pod back into a re-entry vehicle; maybe a replacement computer for the package, preprogrammed for descent to Brazil . . . BTE must have planned all this out well in advance. Then enormous cranes would pull *Willy Ley* erect, where it would be mated to its new solid fuel boosters and external tanks. That process would take a little over a hundred hours. Finally, the entire assembly would be moved to the launch pad for final systems check and fueling, and launched. Total—"Call it a hundred fifty hours."

"You may collect Diaz on the next pass. Will that cost you fuel?"

"It won't maroon us. We have to be very careful, though."

Diaz laughed, an ugly sound. "We cannot

even *see* this cable, this *thread* my employers want. Yet it supports a spacecraft weighing many tons and hangs it from thin air! Who would believe such a thing?"

"Anyone with a serious interest in the space program."

Correro moved up to take Diaz's seat. He looked out at the gray mass of the cable pod—dwindling now, pulling ahead in its pendulum swing—and chuckled. "You think that you are the great man because you know all of these things." He waved his arms at the panels and dials surrounding them, and out the windows to the stars beyond. He shook his head. "Poor foolish man. Do you really think that these things matter? No, you are nothing but a driver, a highly-paid, educated servant. The real decisions, the real power will always be with the men who understand money. And we will always own men like you."

There was a time when Burgess would have smashed Correro in the face instantly, obliterating the shit-eating grin in a welter of blood and shattered teeth. But through the years the wild, fierce fire had dimmed to a steady glow and he sat, hearing the words echo in his head, and did nothing but knot his moist hands into fists.

He looked at the clock. Three hours since *Willy Ley* left the arena, two and a half since Diaz had jammed the cable. Were there laws covering space piracy? The only spot of amusement in the whole nasty affair was the length of time it had taken Ground Control to figure out what *Anansi* was doing—and tell Correro.

Anansi was using the tidal effect to move without rockets.

Burgess hoped he had been able to keep his face straight. BTE Ground Control had talked to Correro for nearly ten minutes in Portugese, and Correro hadn't understood anything. Finally, Correro had thrust the microphone at Burgess and the harried man on the ground had spit abominably pronounced, highly technical English at him in the desperate hope that Burgess could then explain it to Correrro.

On the thrust of a pair of limpet motors, *Anansi*'s crew had set the ship moving slightly lower and slower than the cable pod. Dropping, *Anansi* had picked up velocity and drawn ahead by the time the slack cable drew taut. The tension pulled the cable pod forward-and-down, the Shuttle backward-and-up. Slowing, *Anansi* had dropped (raising its velocity); accelerating, the cable pod had climbed to higher orbit (and slowed). The two masses pulled apart, unreeling more cable while still maintaining the tension that pulled backward on *Anansi*, forward on the cable pod . . .

The peculiar motion would stymie any attempt the BTE Shuttles might make to match orbits. Granted, the center of mass of the system was in a classic Newtonian orbit.

But nothing was *at* that point except a stretch of invisibly thin thread. The pod and *Anansi* were not in orbits at all; they were hanging from the cable's endpoints, still pulling apart. Presently *Anansi* would be low enough to cut loose and fall.

And Burgess was saying, "Wait, wait, I don't understand. It's like lifting yourself by your own bootstraps, it can't—Hah? But if the Shuttle is being pulled *back*, how can it go *faster?*" Holding the laughter inside himself while the BTE man shouted that anything in a lower orbit *had* to move faster, you idiot! getting louder and less coherent until he was screaming in Portugese, words Burgess hadn't heard even in the bordellos. Burgess had finally hung up, then tried to explain to Correro, using a light-pointer and one of the screens to draw diagrams.

What a grand joke! And the best part of it was that not Correro, nor Olivera, nor Diaz nor anyone else knew for certain that Burgess had held out on them.

"Eric." Diaz's voice was blurring a bit with distance. "Is *Anansi* moving?"

"I'll see." Burgess swung the radar system down, and presently found *Anansi* against a limb of the Earth. He watched. Presently he said, "Not moving, not that I can see. Why?"

"The line. It's vibrating. That scrap of cloth is trembling. I thought maybe . . . *My God, wh—?*" There was a blast of static, then a dull machine squeal.

"Ricardo?" Burgess cut in the noise suppressors and got nothing—no breathing, no words. Correro was at the window beside him, straining to see, but the cable pod was not much more than a dot. "Damn! At the very least, his radio's gone out."

"What happened?" A touch of genuine panic tautened Correro's slender face.

"*Anansi* has counterattacked. Somehow. They must have got somebody up that line."

"But—but *how?* It's over three hundred kilometers!"

Burgess shook his head appreciatively. "However he did it, it's a hell of an achievement." The static over the line was an irritation now, no longer interesting. He reached out and flicked the headphone off.

Correro seethed. "You must go out and kill that man!"

"Have to catch him first. Here—" Burgess tapped the radar readout. "The cable pod's rising too fast. *Anansi*'s man must have kicked out the wedge."

"Take us back."

"Yeah. Buckle in." Fuel supply be damned, he couldn't abandon Diaz . . . though he was half-sure Diaz must be dead. A touch of the CNS motors lined *Brasilia*'s nose with its now dot-sized target. Burgess fired the main motors, and watched the fuel registers while the Shuttle's orbit altered. When radar said that the cable pod was approaching, he cut the motors.

He would graze the cable pod's path, now, and continue outward unless he used yet more fuel. *Brasilia* carried the big supplementary tanks used for longer missions; they filled half the cargo bay. But he could still be marooned. Like *Anansi*, but with no cable to save them. Lost in the sky with Correro for company until *Willy Ley* could rescue him.

"We must kill him, or everything is ruined!"

Burgess *tsk'd* unsympathetically. "Not: 'We must go out and rescue Ricardo Diaz'? Where's your sense of priorities?"

Correro's face darkened, and his lips worked in silence. Then: "Diaz is unimportant, in comparison with the cable."

"That's a pretty nasty way to screw your partner."

Correro made a spitting motion. "He was as ignorant as . . . he knew as little as you." Burgess enjoyed watching the perspiration bead on Correro's forehead. "Now . . . you must go out there, and . . . rescue Diaz, and kill the man who had attacked him. Yes."

"No." Burgess scratched at his beard, then held up a hand, ticking off fingers. "First, I was hired to fly, not fight. Second, the mission was a *rescue* mission, and I'll be damned if I'll be a party to murder." He bent another finger down and leaned closer to Correro. "And third, I don't like you, never have. I don't like your nasty little smile, and I don't like your breath—it smells like you've been eating raw snails. But I can tell you what I *do* like. What I like is the fact that there isn't a damned thing you can do about it."

Correro leaned away from Burgess as if the pilot were an angry cobra. Shock froze his eyes for a few seconds, then his hand plunged into his flight jacket emerging with a gas-driven dart gun. "Do not tell me that the bullet will go through you and pierce the hull of this craft. That would be a lie. Now—you will either do as I say, or I will kill you. Now."

An unfeigned smile wound its way onto Burgess' mouth. Almost he laughed aloud. "And who will fly you home?"

"I—I'll wait for *Willy Ley* to come back . . ." The words trailed away, as Correro was remembering how very far he was from Sao Luis.

"Right," Burgess said coldly. "And what will you do if our friend out there decides to attach a few ounces of explosive to our windows? I wouldn't put it past them. On the whole, *Anansi*'s crew has proven damned resourceful." He stood, and moved carefully over to Correro, whose face had bled from ruddy to ashen. The man seemed about to collapse. "I tell you what, Correro," he said. "*You* go out there and kill our intruder. You'll find a suit and mobility pack on the lower deck. I'm sure you've had an hour or more of free fall training. You'll figure it out." The two were close together now, almost breathing each other's breath, and Correro's finger was trembling on the trigger.

"We're almost close enough now. You'll have to move fast," Burgess said. "And by the way, Correro. Whether you stay here, or go out into the sky—" He pointed at the window. When Correro's gaze followed the gesture Burgess moved, twisting the gun hand inward with his right hand, punching Correro brutally hard with his left. The BTE man bounced into the wall, eyes crossing, and Burgess hit him again, in the stomach. Then, almost casually, he returned to his seat and watched Correro gag. When the man was well enough to hear, Burgess finished the thought. "Where was I? Oh, yes. No matter *where* you are, don't ever point a gun at a man unless you're ready to use it. And, friend, you weren't ready."

Correro tried to find something to say, but the hatred and fear clogged his throat, and only inarticulate sounds forced their way through. Finally, he climbed down from the control level, and closed the grill behind him.

Burgess examined the knuckles on his left hand. They were bruised and beginning to ooze blood. But by *God* it had been worth it!

Seventeen

THIN EDGE

The cable was running freely again. Thomas De Camp stood on the tail of the cable pod, looking up, trying to find a scrap of bright cloth against a gibbous Earth. He couldn't. Even in these few seconds of freedom, the cable had carried it too far.

Mission accomplished.

He wondered how long he had to live.

At best, he would run out of air. It was really as simple as that: his recycler could only handle his carbon dioxide output for another hour or so. Hypoxia wasn't a terrible way to die. If he didn't watch his gauges, he might not even realize that he was dying, and merely slip away into delirium and the final sleep with a minimum of discomfort.

But before that happened . . . *Brasilia* could

have a nasty ace up her sleeve. How many men did she carry? If the Brazilian offer of a ride home had been genuine, then they must have had room to house the full crew of *Anansi:* four, including Stonecypher. That put three men aboard now, to bring their homeward load to seven, the maximum for a Shuttle . . . unless *Brasilia* carried a pressure can in her cargo bay. That would put his calculations into the toilet. An army could swarm all over him at any moment.

He sighed, and looked up into swirled patches of white cloud and blue ocean. Earth was close enough, big enough to serve as a noonday sky, but for the blackness around the rim. Day overhead and night underfoot, and an arc of night encroaching on the day. *Anansi* was up there somewhere, invisibly remote, lost in her own battles, beyond the reach of his suit radio, gone forever. "I hope you make it, sweetheart." His eyes picked out patterns in the clouds: there a cluster of mushrooms, there a mountain range seen from his father's private plane.

And there was Janet's smile, a thing of sunshine and light rain, glowing at him from the sky. "I love you," he said, and blushed in the dark, wishing that he had been able to bring himself to say that to her, in person, in time.

The clumsy fluttering of a suited leg caught his attention. The lone bandit was less than ten yards away, clamped to a climbing rung by a cable gripper around his airhose.

Thomas had dropped squarely on him, knocked him cold as a cucumber; had barely stopped him from tumbling bonelessly into the starry night. Thomas' cable grippers had him moored to the rung before he woke enough to struggle.

At that, the bandit could give thanks that Thomas had spent the last thirty kilometers or so decelerating. That was tricky. The tackle had held him to the cable with a loop of more cable, when orbital dynamics were trying to pull him away, drop him behind. He'd pushed a block of tungsten carbide into the loop as a friction brake. The cable had etched holes in the block; he'd had to keep moving it as he fell.

Otherwise he would have hit the bandit like a *real* bomb.

At first the bandit had struggled, flailing arms and legs in a helpless jitterbug of panic as he tried to reach the cable grippers. Now ... if it weren't for the intermittent twitch, Thomas would suspect the man was dead.

Nothing to do but wait ...

A white triangle, smaller than a pinhead at first, was growing at the limb of the Earth. *Anansi?* Not bloody likely. *Brasilia* to the rescue. Count on at least one man, armed to the teeth. One, or many; but not two. Two would leave *Brasilia* empty and falling away. Count on *one*.

And what were his options? Thomas hefted

the automatic rifle, empty now, but still a credible bluff. No sane man would risk an impact from one of the explosive shells. He could play for time until . . .

Until his air ran out. No (he shook his head violently) that was no way to think of it. Until *Anansi* was safe!

Any other options? No BTE bandit was likely to have more hours in space than a Falling Angel man. The bandit would be clumsy. He wouldn't have *Brasilia*'s help, either. *Brasilia* couldn't stay alongside.

The pod itself: half of it was starkly outlined in sunlight, the other half as deeply shadowed as the lunar night. Perfect for a deadly game of hide and seek.

He checked his oxygen again. A *short* game—

Brasilia turned as she neared; the cargo bay yawned in his face. *There was no pressure can!* The sun glared into the cargo bay and showed him a man-shape (one!) moving within.

In another minute Thomas could see that the man carried something suspiciously like the rifle *Willy Ley*'s soldier had used to make a shambles of *Anansi*'s cargo bay. Thomas pictured one of those shells impacting with his own body, and a bubble of sour gas expanded painfully in his stomach. He began climbing around to the dark side of the pod, slipping into deep shadow.

Brasilia's soldier rose out of the cargo bay when the Shuttle was fifty meters from the pod. Immense in his sight now, the spacecraft hovered close for a few seconds, then began to drop away again, diminishing as swiftly as she had grown.

Thomas fiddled with his radio; caught something; homed in. The new man was talking under his breath. The few words he could make out were curses, apparently aimed at the backpack itself. Thomas watched from shadow as the man clumsily attempted to change course, falling past the cable pod, coming back too fast, turning, forgetting that it would take jets to slow him . . .

Well well . . . sending out the rookies, were they? Thomas began to hope. He would need to know what the newcomer wanted. The cable, ultimately. And Thomas' life? Or the crippled conspirator?

The sun was moving, and he dared not forget where the shadows lay. He swung out to the shadowed side of a fin and climbed out along its length, hidden from the captured bandit. At the end of the fin he extended himself out on one arm to peer back. It felt as if he were holding a ten-kilo weight at arm's length, a slow ache.

Brasilia's warrior reached his ally where Thomas had moored him, just out of reach of the cable. They touched helmets briefly. The newcomer's radio gave Thomas two blurred voices speaking Portugese. Good: Thomas had wondered if his prisoner was alive. The newcomer checked the clamps holding the air hose to the foot rung. He twisted at it, then glared up at the pod. It would be simple to free the man, Thomas reflected, but only for one who could reach around at an angle impossible for the prisoner himself.

Thomas released his grip on the foot rung and wasted a precious burst of fuel floating out into the sunlight. He aimed his rifle squarely at the newcomer's head, and waited to be seen.

From the reaction, a sudden thrashing jerk, Thomas could guess at the look on the man's face: surprise, then panic. His enemy did a slow-motion scramble around the curve of the pod, then cautiously emerged again, this time weapon first, and squeezed off a long burst. A few rounds struck the external skin of the pod, exploding with flashes of light and dust. Thomas was already gone, back on the pod's flank and climbing down toward the nose.

He smiled grimly to himself. Would his clumsy foe see through the bluff? Thomas liked the other side of the question better: could the man *afford* to believe the gun was empty?

In silence, Thomas completed his climb to the bottom of the cable pod. Now he was anchored by two rungs. The shadow of the pod had swung around. It was blacker than black now, blocked from sunlight and Earthlight too. He could hear his enemy's breathing but not see him.

The sound, though: ragged breathing, exertion. Thomas sensed it getting clearer, closer. Not climbing, though. There were no soft, rhythmic grunts to indicate that kind of activity. Even at the tenth of a gee that was effective aboard the cable pod, there should have been some change in the breathing.

Mobility pack then. He bet himself that he could take a quick look. A novice couldn't operate a mobility pack and aim an automatic rifle simultaneously.

He climbed around the shadowed back of the pod, silently thanking the engineers for setting so many rungs into its rock slag surface. He swung from hand to hand as if moving through Falling Angel's jungle gym, and came around into the light just in time to see his enemy approach. The man was drifting slowly down the flank of the pod, jets popping from time to time.

A chill rippled through Thomas' muscles. He hadn't known how ominous the pressure suits could look. Faceless, almost shapelessly inhuman, more like a demon in white than Thomas cared to consider.

For an instant he was frozen in terror, feeling the bullet explode somewhere in his body, hearing his own final, gobbling scream of fear and pain dwindle into vacuum . . .

Then he snapped out of it. His enemy's faceplate was a silvery, reflective oval, but the man beneath was human. Human, and fallible, and mortal, and if Thomas had to die, he was going to take one more of the bastards with him.

As the man dropped past him toward the nose of the pod, Thomas turned loose and used his mobility pack to ascend the sunlit side. Easy: just thrust like hell, brake when you're behind a fin, reach out and grab a rung. Thomas had all the fuel he needed. The bandit would keep reserve fuel to bring himself back to *Brasilia*.

The captive's head turned when Thomas reached him. His faceplate was misted with moist, warm breath. Something wrong with his recycler. The man didn't look the part of a villain; he looked young, and sick, and semi-conscious. Thomas wrung the pity from his mind. How the hell would *he* know what a villain looked like?

Last trump, Dexter. Either this works, or I'll be seeing you. Soon.

Thomas retreated, back onto the shadowed side of a horizontal fin, and hugged himself close against the leading edge. The Earth was a shrinking crescent. Darkness felt good: safe.

He turned up his radio. "This is Thomas De Camp, hailing *Brasilia* crewman. I know that you intend to kill me. I'm warning you," letting hysteria creep into his voice, "if you proceed any further, I will kill your partner." There was no reply, of course. "Don't think I'm bluffing. I've got at least two ways to rupture his suit, and one to smash his faceplate." Still no answer.

Thomas breathed deeply. He couldn't see

the injured man, nor the cable running out on its spool. Where was *Anansi?* How long until she could cut herself free?

He waited. His enemy should be discovering the depth of shadow, thinking it a wonderful place to hide, creeping upward to deal death to *Anansi's* champion. "I'm warning you," Thomas said heavily. "Don't try any tricky stuff . . ." He only had to *allow* the hysteria to creep into his voice. His fingers were on the mobility pack keys. If he saw the bandit in the wrong place he would jet away at once and try to dodge behind the hull.

He heard puffing in his radio. This time the bandit was climbing.

There: very close, climbing the hull with one hand on his gun, a faceless, pudgy shape barely visible in shadow. He climbed past Thomas and kept moving.

Thomas said, "Forty seconds, mister. I'm waiting to hear from you." He saw the man pause, heard his breath sobbing through the filters. The helmeted head turned this way and that, but didn't see the curved edge of Thomas' helmet. He kept moving.

Thomas swung beneath the fin and climbed after him. He said, "Ever see explosive decompression? Your friend will look like someone stuck an air hose into his guts and switched it up 'full'—" Was that colorful enough? The manshape froze, then continued its jerky, one-armed climb. The ion tech climbed after him, gaining.

Correro transferred the gun to his left hand. He could guess what that would do to his accuracy; but strained muscles were shrieking in his back, left shoulder, left arm. He continued climbing, past the fins, using only his right arm. The mobility pack threw him off, pulled him backward.

He slowed. Here was the curve of the cable pod's tail ... and *Anansi*'s man would be beyond the curve, standing or crouched, possibly with an elbow crooked around Diaz's throat. Looking in an unknown direction. Correro's heartbeat thundered in his ears. He surged over the curve gun-and-helmet first and saw Diaz still anchored to the rung. Where was the American? Correro completed his motion—too hard, so that for a moment he floated—and dropped next to Diaz. *Where was the American?*

Diaz hadn't reacted. Sick? Dead? At least his airhose was intact. Correro had almost whooped for joy to find Diaz alive. Now he was concerned. Diaz's well-being was precious to him. Was Diaz in shape to fly a Shuttle back to Brazil?

Where was the American? Fled in fear! Correro gave a harsh bark of derision. He knew it—the American's gun was empty, it was a bluff. Now he could jam the cable, and call for *Brasilia*.

The rest would be easy—*if* Diaz was in shape to fly *Brasilia*. That would mean that the pig Burgess had no further business sucking up good air. Correro would take great pleasure in cutting Burgess' throat, working the blade in until it grated at the cartilage. Correro's mouth and nose still stung from the Shuttle pilot's blow, and the thought of bloody vengeance helped dull the tickle of fear at the back of his neck. He reached into his belt and extracted a sliver of laboratory sapphire, and the hammer necessary to wedge it into the cable opening.

He could see the cable, a thread of silver lit by the sun, reaching infinitely high, to Earth itself, it seemed. He moved forward.

Something massive slammed into his back. He tried desperately to turn around, and couldn't. He heard: "Have a closer look, you bastard—" He tried to lean backward, to dig his feet in. His feet flailed in midair.

The cable was unreeling at better than a hundred kilometers an hour at that point. At first Correro felt no more pain than that of a paper cut. The cable didn't tug at flesh or spray blood about like a bandsaw blade would have. It cut far more neatly. But air spewed from around him, and his body felt like it was exploding, and his eyes crossed as they followed the silver thread. It was inside his faceplate.

Thomas had used the empty gun as a lever, shoving it under the base of the bandit's mobility pack and thrusting forward and up.

Fear and rage had put all his considerably strength behind the maneuver.

Too hard! The thread was inches from his eyes when he braked himself. He stared in horror at the two halves of his gun, at cut metal surfaces that gleamed like mirrors. He hurled them violently into the sky. Only an iron act of will kept his stomach from throwing unbreathable vomit into his helmet.

The bandit? Thomas looked for him, and found him overhead, a dark blob rising in a fog of gasses. The cable hadn't turned him loose yet; it was still reeling out through his corpse, its minute friction pulling him upward.

What now? "Mission accomplished," he muttered. Nothing now, except die.

Then he heard slow, laconic handclapping, and a dry chuckle. "Very good, whoever you are. You're a very clever man."

Thomas looked around quickly, saw nothing. "Where are you?"

"About twenty kilometers ahead of you, I think."

"Would you be Burgess?"

"None other. Looks like a Mexican standoff, I'd say."

"Brazilian standoff, maybe. And not for long. This is no quick, quiet act of piracy any more. By this time it's all over the news services on Earth. Oyama Construction will have pressured the Japanese consulate into making a formal protest to the Brazilian ambassador. Japanese and American industry supply nearly two-thirds of Brazil's electronics. I doubt Brazil will let this thing go on. You're finished, Burgess. Accessory to attempted piracy, sabotage, and murder."

There was a long silence. The air in Thomas' helmet smelled close and sour. Imagination, he hadn't been out that long . . . but he'd been working himself unmercifully, using up air . . .

"You may not believe this." Burgess sounded a million kilometers away. Where was *Brasilia*? Should be ahead, falling back.

"Believe what?"

"I didn't know about all of this. Not when I took off. I thought it was a legitimate rescue mission." There was a snorting laugh of regret. "I did figure out some of what was going on once I got up here, but I was in pretty deep by then, and that bastard Correro— never mind. From your voice I figure you're still pretty young. Maybe you won't understand this, but Brazil was the only spacegoing nation that would offer me a contract. I just *had* to keep flying . . ." Burgess made a sound like a punctured balloon whistling air. "Oh, what the hell. It's all blown now, why bother talking about it? How's Diaz?"

"I'd say he's injured. He's still breathing."

"Good."

"Burgess, weren't you still with NASA when you went to Brazil?"

"Yeah, but I would have been grounded in

two years. Brazil needed someone to fly, and train, and offered to let me fly until I was sixty. An extra five years! I felt like a condemned man given a last minute reprieve. Can you understand that?" Burgess was losing control of his voice, and Thomas found himself a believer. Janet was right. This was a man who loved The Dream as much as any of them. A foolish man, perhaps, but not a bad one.

Or had the thickening air, and the wish to believe, dulled his mind? *What does it matter? What is there to lose?* "I can understand that." Thomas checked his air gauge and found it edging into the red. Not much time left at all.

"You can't go home, Burgess. The Brazilian government will make you a scapegoat. Can't you see the headlines? 'Renegade American pilot indicted in piracy scheme.' BTE might even kill you to cover their tracks."

"I . . . doubt that."

"Feel free." Thomas was gulping for air now, and his chest was beginning to ache. *Relax! Calm! Give the recycler a chance to keep up.* "I'll tell you this for sure, you'll never fly again."

In the silence that followed he spotted a dim, distant winged shape. *Brasilia,* ahead of him, approaching tail first.

"Yeah, I know. Listen, I'm a kilometer away and closing. You're the only one who can save Diaz. Your life for his. You take him and you jump. I'll pick you up."

That easy? Of course he was right, they'd have to jump. Jump, and trust the pilot of the killer ship. Thomas pictured two corpses, abandoned evidence, lost in the sky. But he could make it a better bet.

"Burgess. Maybe there's a way out. You can come over to Falling Angel. Brazil will never make reparations for the damage done by her Shuttles. All right, then, we'll take one of her Shuttles in trade."

"My God. You're serious, aren't you?"

"Dead serious. There's an ion drive on its way here: *Michael*, I'd guess. We can push you back to lunar orbit. We'll have to examine all of the evidence in the case, but if you're clean, I think that Falling Angel Enterprises will be glad to have you. And one more thing—there will be a lot of orbit-to-orbit runs. No heavy gee-stresses. I think you can count on an extra five years over what Brazil promised you. Maybe more, if you've got a healthy heart." Thomas was no longer sure that he was making sense. His lungs strained at the soupy air; his head whirled with hypoxia.

There was a tremulous, childlike quality to Burgess' voice. "I've got to retrofire. Stand by. Can you promise—"

"I can't promise anything!" Thomas screamed it. "All I can say is that if you're clean, and we can prove it, we'll want you. And if you're not clean, to hell with you. Just, just . . . let me die in peace."

There was another pause. But *Brasilia*,

closer now, was blazing at her tail. Accelerating to match with the cable pod. Burgess gave a painfully long, drawn-out sigh. "You can jump any time now, but *take Diaz*. He wasn't part of this mess either. What's your name, fella?"

"De Camp. Thomas De Camp. Why the hell does it matter?"

"I don't know. Because you're good, you really are. Come aboard and we'll wait for your ion drive ship. Then you can take us both to Falling Angel and put us on trial. I'd rather take my chances with Lunatics than those marionette judges in Brazil. I'm not sure we've still got fuel to re-enter anyway. Come on, move!"

Thomas was already disentangling Diaz. The man was still alive, which was more than Thomas would be if he didn't get fresh air soon . . . no! Air or not, he was going to stay alive on sheer will power, if need be. "You've got a deal. Burgess?"

"Yeah?"

"You're right. I'm good!"

Eighteen

THE DESCENT OF ANANSI

One of the cable-reinforced staples gave way and ripped free of the cargo bay. *Anansi* dropped like a piano. Marion, braced against what must be a fifth of a gee by now, found he had sprung out to the end of his short safety tether. Then the cable pulled taut against the next staple and *Anansi* surged up at him. He struck the floor on hands and knees, a jolting four-point landing—and a second staple flicked silently past his helmet.

The next staple held.

"Getting rough," he said. "We lost a couple of stitches."

"Are you hurt?"

"No. Worried." He peered through the hazy light at the zigzag pattern of cable and staples that anchored *Anansi* at the end of a now-static cable. "If we lose about ten more we might rip ourselves loose, which is fine. But this kind of jerking around could snap the cable somewhere in the middle, and that isn't good at all. We've got to cut the cable *now*."

"Right. Any luck?"

"I'm still looking."

Much of the debris, solid and liquid, had been left kilometers back. It was easier to see his way around in the bay. The damage from the exploding rounds had been terrible. Marion had been re-lashing broken crates into place with spare line while he searched. Still, frayed edges and leaking contents dappled the interior of the Shuttle bay.

"The cutters *have* to be there."

Marion remembered the assault, with glowing shards of plastic crating material whirling off into space, gears and liquids and bundles of fiber and entire pods floating free, disappearing. "I'm not so sure any more. We opened one crate of cable grippers and took two out, and Thomas took them both with him. Now the crate is gone, and why would there be two crates of cable grippers? Why not just a bigger crate?"

"Oh, God, what a mess. At least . . . Tommy is safe. I never expected that."

"Yeah! Better than that. *We won*. No matter *what* happens now, the cable's strung out over fourteen hundred kilometers, and *nobody's* going to bring it back to Earth in that condition. Now I only have to find a way to cut it."

"Just stay safe. We don't need to prove we're heroes. We've done that."

He chuckled. "Aye aye, Cap'n."

What was there to sever Stonecypher Cable? There was sure as hell no way to *break* it. It would slice through any sharp implement on *Anansi*, he was sure of that. What did that leave? What did Thomas have among his tools? Pliers? Soldering tools? *A torch?*

Marion made his way back to the airlock, stopping every so often to move the end of his safety tether. *Anansi* was steady as a rock except when a staple ripped away. The cable must be under tremendous tension. It *would* snap, no telling where, if something weren't done . . .

He cycled through the lock, unscrewed his helmet, didn't bother removing the rest. There *ought* to be a torch. This was the locker where tools were kept for minor repairs . . . *hah!* Cutting torch. He shook it and the tanks sloshed: full.

He paused to replace his oxygen tank before going out. Last bottle. *Anansi*'s air recycler would last another ten hours, maybe, and then they'd be breathing the oxygen in their pressure suits until *that* ran out.

Light was dim in the cargo bay, an attempt to save power for the air recycling plant, but by watching the staples he knew exactly where the cable was at all times. He didn't want to walk into the thing. He remembered Thomas' description of what had happened to the BTE enforcer, and his blood ran cold.

How many had died for this cable? Four? Five? And what would become of *Anansi* if Dexter Stonecypher had done his job too well? Would they hang in Earth's upper atmosphere forever, a bizarre monument to the technical wizardry of Falling Angel?

He attached his safety line to a grip and popped the torch on, a pencil-thin cone of incandescent gas projecting its seven-inch length from the tip.

"Janet, I'm about to try a torch. If it actually cuts through, we're going to take a hell of a jolt and drop *fast*. I suggest that we close the bay doors about halfway, now, so it won't take as long to seal them when we make our descent."

"Aye aye, Marion. I'll leave the line open."

He felt the floor vibrating, and great shadows closed across the moon. He asked, "Just where do we want to be when the cable parts?"

"Good thinking. Let's see, we usually get almost a full orbit after retrofire, but . . . we'd be entering slower this time, so . . . we're passing over Asia . . . give it another five minutes, then go."

The stars were creeping across the black opening in the bay doors. Marion, trying to rest, found himself looking at Stonecypher's pressure suit. Something like a fat, gray, distorted mushroom stood out below Stonecypher's ribs. What could have caused . . .?

Shit. A bullet must have exploded there, and

blood and flesh had foamed out. Marion whispered, "Closed-coffin ceremony, Dexter. I'd launch you overboard and give you a meteor's funeral, but I can't. You're evidence. Anyway, we got him."

"Marion? What was that?"

He jumped. "Just talking to a friend, Janet."

A torch *ought* to cause single-crystal iron fibers to lose their stability. It had better. They couldn't be rescued, neither from above nor below. Hell, they'd planned it that way! If all of the staples ripped loose under cable tension, *Anansi* would fall. They would enter the atmosphere at less than the normal re-entry speed: just as well, given the Shuttle's chewed-up condition. Of course, once the cable was parted they'd have *no* further choice about where they landed. If they timed it right they might even reach Japan . . .

But Marion's intuition saw staples snapping loose one after another, shock waves traveling along the cable until whiplash snapped pieces away at the far end. Until *Anansi* entered the atmosphere trailing hundreds of kilometers of lethal thread. He imagined it falling across the city, in loops around buildings and cars and children.

Time. Marion thought of starting at the furthest staple, then changed his mind: he didn't want to be near the next metal strip to give way. It could jump up and crack his faceplate. He shuffled back four staples, and got to work.

In the intense light of the torch, the cable showed as a dark hairline. He applied the flame where the cable crossed the staple.

Like the filament of a lamp, the strand began to glow, first a dull red, then brightening to an eye-numbing white like the core of the torch's flame. The zone of white spread along the cable to make a five-inch strand of glowing line.

Marion waited. He was beginning to notice the heat. He couldn't see the waste gasses from the torch, but they swirled around him, eating at his suit, defeating his cooling system.

Another staple snapped free, and *Anansi* dropped under him. Reflexively he switched the torch off. The staple: he could see it embedded in one of the bay doors. The cable pulled taut—and he saw a glare-white thread disappearing between the bay doors. The floor hit him and bounced him back to the end of his tether and left him floating.

"—Falling!" he screamed, in a reflex that true astronauts weren't supposed to have. Then, "We're falling! Janet, close the bay doors! I did it!"

Her voice was ecstatic. "You sure as hell did! Aye aye, closing cargo bay doors. Get back in here and out of that suit and into your chair. We'll be in the atmosphere in ten minutes."

He felt himself being tugged gently toward the nose, away from the ladder, as he climbed to the command level. Traces of atmosphere, already. Never in his life had he stripped out of a pressure suit faster. He hadn't even stopped to put slippers on.

Janet had slipped coolly into her pilot's personna. Her body was relaxed but poised, hands moving smoothly and confidently on the controls. Her face looked old and her eyes were red and puffy, but the only sign of discomfiture was the puzzled tone as she spoke into the microphone.

"—can't land on Okinawa? Why not?" She snarled as the answer came back. Marion eased into his chair, buckled himself in swiftly, and fitted on his headphones.

A cultured Japanese voice was speaking in carefully measured tones. "—American embassy has verified it. The landing strip in the Ryukyu Islands is under lease to NASA and the American Air Force. They will allow you to land, but your craft and cargo will be confiscated, and you may be arrested."

Marion groaned. "So now we're the bandits. Jesus!" His eyes were checking readouts. *Anansi*'s shielding was beginning to warm up in the thin breath of Earth's atmosphere.

Janet set her mouth. Her golden hair framed a face frozen in controlled anger. "What do you advise, Oyama?"

"Your best option seems to be Tokyo International. We have emergency arrangements with them. They have Tactical Air Navigation, and a VHF omnidirectional radio beacon. I suggest you allow us to program your guidance computer for those coordinates."

She pondered for a second and a half, then smiled grimly. "Tsk. No choice." She turned to her copilot. "Marion, assist the programming. We'll be landing in Tokyo, believe it or not." A quick look at the guidance screen told her that they were starting to cross the Tibetan Plateau, still better than eight hundred miles from Japan. She could make it. They had the altitude, and landing would be easier than NASA's standard Abort Once Around mode.

Anansi flew with a tremor and a tendency to pull to the left. She checked the external temperature, and nodded silently. It was up to 2000 degrees and climbing. The near-vacuum was growing denser. The heat shielding would be glowing cherry red, the nose of the ship shrouded in an envelope of flame. Blast-torn tiles would be falling from the tail. She could feel the ruptured OMS tanks in the shuddering of the craft, in *Anansi's* hairline loss of stability. Shards of metal would be melting.

She *would not* fail. Marion had done his part. Thomas (Thomas!) had risked everything to do his. And dear dead Dexter Stonecypher had won a greater victory than he could have imagined. Not one link in the chain had failed. It was her turn to produce.

A stubby-winged fireball, *Anansi* dropped over the Tibetan Plateau, toward distant Japan.

Nineteen

TRANSITIONS

Josef Navarres, of the legal firm of Navarres, Navarres, Gomez and Shapiro, closed a hastily-prepared manilla file folder and peered across his desk at his client.

It was difficult to believe that this man was the same Jorge Xavier he had dealt with for so many years. The shoulders were no longer square. His hair was stringy, untended. His eyes seemed weak, watery, and without real focus. He might not have slept in days. And small wonder.

"I believe," Navarres said, leaning back in his chair meditatively, "that the file states the situation clearly, Mr. Xavier. You have criminal and civil action being levied against you in local, federal, and international courts."

Xavier nodded like a man who didn't actually understand at all. His once-handsome face seemed drained of blood and life. He heard Navarro's words as through a deadening fog.

"First, of course, are the charges that you bribed officials of the Brazilian military, and used government vehicles in an act of piracy which resulted in the loss of several lives."

"If I had succeeded," Xavier said dully, barely recognizing his own voice, "they would have taken my tax money and let it go at that."

Navarres smiled noncommitally. Xavier was probably right, but what of it? "Be that as it may, Colonel Olivera has made a full confession of his complicity, apparently an attempt to save himself from a firing squad. If it is any comfort, I doubt he'll succeed."

"Pity."

"Indeed. Now: Oyama Construction, acting on its own and in behalf of Falling Angel Enterprises, is suing BTE and its Board of Directors on approximately twenty-three counts of piracy, theft, murder . . . but you know of these."

Xavier nodded without speaking. His tongue felt thick and gluey.

"The United States government has protested the misuse of the shuttle vehicles they sold Brazil, and are postponing shipments of fuel and parts until a full investigation is completed. Their position seems to be that a branch of their government has been attacked: to wit, Falling Angel." Xavier's eyes did come up at that, and he grimaced. Navarres said, "This, along with the loss of the shuttle *Brasilia*, will cost Brazil around seventy million dollars, which will be subtracted from BTE's assets.

"Of course, your personal funds have been frozen pending the outcome of the various suits, and President Castellon of BTE has obtained a court order barring you from trespassing on any property belonging to the company."

Navarres opened the folder again and browsed for a moment. "Edson Da Silva has already fled the country, and Lucio Giorgi is presently in a hospital in connection with heart problems. Apparently he has offered to make a full confession in exchange for a promise of leniency."

"Yes." Xavier scratched at his face as if pursuing an invisible insect. "I would expect that."

"Finally, your wife has filed for divorce. I think you might agree that that is the least of your problems. Now, Mr. Xavier." Navarres leaned forward, the light from the window behind him forming a blurry halo. "What do you propose to do? Establishing a bond for your release has taxed the resources of my firm, and I would like to know how you propose to repay us. I am afraid that if some arrangement cannot be made we will not be able to represent you in what will doubtless be a protracted and expensive series of legal hearings."

Xavier opened his mouth and closed it without saying a word. He fought to find some rock to stand on, some island of sanity in the midst of the confusion. Navarres' face seemed to recede from view, lost in a fog of doubt. Where had he failed? How? He had been so careful, so very cautious.

He stared blankly at his fingernails, shifting them slightly, watching the overhead lights gleaming off in pinpoint glitter patterns. He barely heard the telephone ring, hardly noticed the death's head look that came over Navarres as he spoke quietly into the receiver.

"That was building security, Mr. Xavier. They have arrested a man in the underground parking garage. He was attaching an explosive device to the ignition of your car. They said he had a message for you. 'Tell Xavier that Hoveida can wait.'"

"I see." Xavier sank into his seat, body feeling cramped and numb.

"Security has informed the police, of course, and you will have a police escort from now on, so . . . if you were thinking of taking a vacation somewhere . . ." He shrugged. "In any case, they've disconnected the bomb. It was approximately one kilo of high explosive, and would certainly have killed you."

As from the bottom of a pit Xavier saw and heard his attorney speak. He pulled himself upright and folded his hands neatly in his lap. A wry smile tugged his mouth as he faced Navarres. "A pity," he said blandly.

Viewed from the side, the shuttle-and-ion-drive assembly might have been some huge magical misshapen moth. The ion drive craft would have been its torso; its rectangular solar panels would serve as wings, and the Shuttle *Brasilia* as its swollen lower abdomen. Soft, deep violet beams would be spreading out from the creature's ion-motor eyes. If one's perception were impossibly fine there were also delicate antennae, reaching seven hundred kilometers to either side. The creature of space would be flying backward, in a slow spiral outward from Earth.

So Thomas De Camp saw it in his imagination. He was in the bubble-igloo aboard *Michael*, Falling Angel's ion drive tug, and he was alone and at peace. Problems remained, but they would be trivial next to what he had lived through.

Burgess had proved enthusiastically cooperative; Diaz at least tractable. Thomas hadn't even considered not sleeping. He'd slept like a brick aboard *Brasilia*, and wakened alive, and eaten and tended his wounds and slept again.

For three days *Michael* had swept inward from the Moon on its column of flensed cesium atoms. The ion drive tug had matched orbits with *Brasilia* thirty hours after *Anansi* made her gaudy landing at Tokyo X.

Tim Connors was an exuberantly cheerful man, short and round and as soft as Guiness was hard. *Michael*'s cramped igloo had nearly driven him nuts. He seemed joyfully mad when he entered *Brasilia*, just because of the chance to stretch his legs. The bizarre circumstances became masked with a kind of forced cameraderie.

In that spirit they had gone to work. Connors and Thomas and Burgess fitted *Gabriel*'s flat nose against *Brasilia*'s belly in forty minutes' time. They had cut the cable free of its pod with one flash of a heavy-duty laser. What was *that* doing mounted on *Gabriel*'s hull? "Fleming insisted. I can guess what he had in mind," Connors said. "Laser cannon for the next wave of bandits."

They had cruised inward, pushing *Brasilia*, to the approximate center of mass of the cable. Thomas' two cable grippers had served to lock onto the cable. They had backed into position, *very* carefully, and welded the handles of the grippers to either side of *Michael*'s tail. Total expenditure: ten hours, and all of the ingenuity Thomas could muster.

Now the cable stretched out to either side, held in a nearly straight line by tidal effects, while *Gabriel* towed it toward lunar orbit. The configuration was extremely stable, with the Earth-tide holding the cable nearly rigid. For a time they had even left *Gabriel* untended.

And the party atmosphere persisted. Even

Diaz caught it. In a gravity field Diaz would have been flat on his back, forbidden to move a muscle. In free fall, with Velcro slippers for anchors, he could move; but he moved as if his guts were Venetian glass. If Thomas came too near he would flinch, then cry out at what the tensing muscles had done to him. But Tim Connors would have none of that; he presently had Thomas and Diaz next to each other in the kitchen, taking turns as they told the tale of that epic flight.

The time came when Thomas needed solitude. He offered to spell Connors in the igloo aboard *Michael*, and Connors had accepted in haste . . .

A dull buzzing sound dragged him back from a bottomless well of peace, and he swatted at the air feebly before coming to his senses. He checked over the control readouts, finding everything in order, and stretched as well as he could: his arms easily brushed both sides of the bubble. He flicked on the radio, yawning. "De Camp here. Is that you, Connors?"

"The same. How was your nap?"

"Cramped, but I bet you know about that already. I've promised my body I'll give it a full workout as soon as we get to Falling Angel."

"Six days. I hope your body trusts you that long."

"Don't smirk. Five hours from now, you and I start trading shifts in the bubble. I think you've gotten your kinks out by now."

"Maybe. Listen, you've got a line from Earth. Tokyo, to be exact. I told them you were too busy to be disturbed—"

"Sadist!" A flush of excitement washed through him, drowning out the fatigue and discomfort. "If it's a lady, patch her through."

"Aye aye—and, De Camp, if she goes sour on you, *our* deal still holds, right?"

"Agreed. Now put her *through*, dammit." It seemed to take an eternity for the whistles and clicks to resolve into recognizable words. He spoke before it had finished. "Darling?"

"I didn't know you cared, lover boy," Marion chuckled.

"Careful, this is an open line. How are things on the dirt? Did you like your reception in Tokyo?"

"Thomas, we were *heroes!* Listen, they were still taxiing 767s and private planes out of the way when we touched down. I'll tell you, Janet handled that bird like a brain surgeon cutting on her only child. They had to rope the crowds back, and even that didn't work. The reporters were all over us, snapping pictures, burning themselves on the heat tiles—"

"Any casualties?"

"Only *Anansi.* Maybe some museum will take her. The motor section looks chewed and half-digested. One of the motors fell off on the way down and we never felt it. The air brake flaps on the vertical fin didn't open either. I thought we'd roll forever. Then we didn't have the refrigeration truck to squirt freon in, so the re-entry heat leaked in and burned out all the electronics. Aside from that . . ." He trailed off, and an unspoken word passed over the miles: *Dexter*. Marion cleared his throat. "Anyway. Oyama had to fight like hell to keep the Japanese government from turning me over to the American Embassy. My cover's blown, of course. I can't very well claim I wasn't aboard *Anansi* when my picture is spread across every newspaper on Earth. Janet and I have been debriefed, examined, interviewed, shot full of nerve tonic and stuck on slabs to sleep it off."

"Don't I remember something about an inheritance? Has that been screwed up?"

"No opinion. I can't make myself care. *Life* and the *National Enquirer* and half a dozen Japanese vidzines are bidding to pay serious money for the story of the first space hijacking. We're talking to Playboy Films and MGM. Hey. Do you think a bright, handsome young stud could make it in California?"

"If his ego could fit under the Golden Gate, sure. Marion. I *love* talking to you, but why don't you get yourself off the line and put my wife on before I put an Eskimo curse on you?"

"Oops. Sorry. Just—hey, Thomas. It was good working with you."

"You too. Take care and all of that. Now put her on."

"Listen, our agent wants to represent you too. Full story rights—"

"Put her on."

There was a short scuffle, what sounded like Janet fighting for the microphone, and she came on line. "Tommy?"

"Here, Janet. Everything's fine. How are your Earthlegs?"

"All right. A little wobbly. And *lonesome.*" She lowered her voice a fraction, as if whispering could give them privacy, as if the line weren't as open as the blackness between them. Thomas twisted in his bubble and looked back at Earth's glowing blue disk, filling a quarter of his sky. "Tommy, I ..." he heard something suspiciously like a sniffle, but before he could say anything she had it straightened out. "I'm supposed to convey the congratulations and appreciation of Oyama Construction and Retsudo Oyama particularly."

"Aren't they mad about the cable?"

"Surprisingly, no. They'll have it in a month, and meanwhile they'll be chewing away at BTE in court. If I read it right—what Retsudo *isn't* saying—it'll end with Oyama in control of BTE. Won't that be nice?"

"Well, then. All is well. I just wish ... well, Dexter." He shook himself out of it. "I don't think he'd want us to mourn him just yet. Not while there's still trouble to work out."

"Trouble ...? Oh, well, Tommy. I guess ... there'd be trouble if there were any loose ends, but you'll be off to the Belt now. Won't you?"

Thomas smiled. "Well," he said slowly, "it'll be awhile yet. We'll have to come back for *Gabriel*, and then rebuild it. And then, Tim Connors and I made a little deal. He'll be taking *Gabriel* to the Belt. Seems he wants to go asteroid hopping more than I do. I could use a little vacation. Maybe see Alaska again, if I can work it out with the government."

"Tommy . . . I've never been to Alaska."

"You wouldn't like it. Too cold. And dull. Nothing to do, really, except find someone you love, and hold them tight for body warmth, and try to make up for lost time."

"Tommy . . . are the nights really six months long?"

"You know better than that. It isn't close enough to the north pole. I can find you a couple of seventy-two-hour evenings, though."

"We could make it *seem* like six months."

"I'll be back in about three weeks, and then we can talk about it."

"Tommy . . . can you say it? Just this once? I need to hear it."

"Say what?" He reached out and squiggled the radio switch. "We're picking up some interference here—I'd better sign off now."

"Please . . . just this once."

"Sorry, gotta go now. The frammistat is acting up."

"The what?"

"The framigasinat."

"Tommy, are you crazy? What did you say?"

"I said that I love you, and I always have." Silence on the other end of the line. "I love you, and you're the most wonderful thing in my life, and you will never have to fight to get me to say it again."

She *was* crying now. "You mean that, don't you."

"I tell you what. Hang on for three weeks, then find out for yourself how much I mean it."

"I'll hang on. Goodby, Tommy."

He mouthed *I love you* silently at the microphone, then broke the connection. Staring out at an uninteresting view of the black-tiled underside of *Brasilia*, he said, "This is going to be a slow three weeks."

GORDON R. DICKSON

POUL ANDERSON
Winner of 7 Hugos and 3 Nebulas

☐	53088-8	CONFLICT	$2.95
	53089-6		Canada $3.50
☐	48527-1	COLD VICTORY	$2.75
☐	48517-4	EXPLORATIONS,	$2.50
☐	48515-8	FANTASY	$2.50
☐	48550-6	THE GODS LAUGHED	$2.95
☐	48579-4	GUARDIANS OF TIME	$2.95
☐	53567-7	HOKA! (with Gordon R. Dickson)	$2.75
	53568-5		Canada $3.25
☐	48582-4	LONG NIGHT	$2.95
☐	53079-9	A MIDSUMMER TEMPEST	$2.95
	53080-2		Canada $3.50
☐	48553-0	NEW AMERICA	$2.95
☐	48596-4	PSYCHOTECHNIC LEAGUE	$2.95
☐	48533-6	STARSHIP	$2.75
☐	53073-X	TALES OF THE FLYING MOUNTAINS	$2.95
	53074-8		Canada $3.50
☐	53076-4	TIME PATROLMAN	$2.95
	53077-2		Canada $3.50
☐	48561-1	TWILIGHT WORLD	$2.75
☐	53085-3	THE UNICORN TRADE	$2.95
	53086-1		Canada $3.50
☐	53081-0	PAST TIMES	$2.95
	53082-9		Canada $3.50

Buy them at your local bookstore or use this handy coupon:
Clip and mail this page with your order

TOR BOOKS—Reader Service Dept.
P.O. Box 690, Rockville Centre, N.Y. 11571

Please send me the book(s) I have checked above. I am enclosing $_____ (please add $1.00 to cover postage and handling). Send check or money order only—no cash or C.O.D.'s.

Mr./Mrs./Miss _____

Address _____

City _____ State/Zip _____

Please allow six weeks for delivery. Prices subject to change without notice.